NOW OR LATER

Dominic looked down at Foche. Blood was coming from his stomach and back. He was a goner. Foche knew it too. Blood bubbling between his lips, he choked out, ''Well, get on with it. You know what has to be done. You wouldn't leave me alive for them to play with, would you?''

Charter Books by Barry Sadler

DESERT MERCENARY

#16

BARRY SADLER

© CHARTER BOOKS, NEW YORK

CASCA #16: DESERT MERCENARY

A Charter Book / published by arrangement with
the author

PRINTING HISTORY
Charter edition/February 1986

ISBN: 0-441-09336-1

Charter Books are published by The Berkley Publishing Group,
200 Madison Avenue, New York, New York 10016.
PRINTED IN THE UNITED STATES OF AMERICA

CHAPTER ONE

Tunis still bore the scars of World War II. In the harbor the hulks of dead ships were serving as breakwaters. From the docks the last survivors of Rommel's Afrika Korps had tried to escape under the guns of the Allied forces. Few made it back to Germany. Most of the shell holes pockmarking the streets had been filled, but many buildings still stood as gutted ruins inhabited only by rats, scorpions, and some occasional human vermin.

Gustof Beidemann sat, contentedly enough on the surface, stuffing his mouth with dates and sweet rice, using his fingers as a spoon. His companion was more silent. The last months had been exceedingly boring. Their last job had been merely that of shotgun riders on convoys taking supplies out to where some American and British companies had been putting up drilling rigs. Not much action, only a plenitude of sun, flies, and bad water when you could get it.

Carl Langers rinsed his mouth with sips of wine grown from French cuttings in Algeria. It was good.

"Gus?"

The chewing stopped only long enough for the bear of a man to quickly respond, "*Ja*?"

"Where do we go from here? Central Africa?"

The bear belched, drawing an appreciative look from the other customers of the harbor-side bistro.

"I don't know. There are the Gulf Emirates. I would prefer them to working in Central Africa. There are too many uncertainties there, and it is not always easy to get your money."

Langers leaned back in the chair of woven reeds. To the north he could see the Mediterranean, the calm blue sea as clear as glass, but the sense of peacefulness that it inspired was only temporary. He had long ago determined that conflict, not peace, was the natural order of man, for peace and calm were always transitory things for Carl Langers aka Casca Rufio Longinus. Since that fateful moment 2,000 years ago when he had sunk his spear into the crucified body of Christ, Casca had been denied the rest of the weary, dying countless times only to wake once again in the world of the living. Eternal death would have been sweet salvation for Casca alias Langers. But he was destined to live the hell of one damned to immortality until the Second Coming would reprieve him.

He and his giant friend would have preferred to be in Algiers, but the memory of that notorious time in the Légion Étrangère there was still too fresh. Too many knew them by sight and old grudges die hard. That had been a bad and bloody time when he and Gus had come back from Indochina after the fall of Dien Bien Phu, a very bad and bloody time. They had taken their discharges as soon as their time was up, not wishing to participate any further in the seemingly random and insane slaughter that had taken place between the French Colonials and the Algerian Nationalists. It was one of those cases where everyone was the bad guy and there was no absolute right or wrong—only the fanatics.

Gus opened his throat to take in a handful of couscous, then farted with satisfaction. Several nearby diners promptly left their tables, meals uneaten.

"Don't be impatient, Carl. Monpelier said he would meet us here and he will. He said only that he would arrive by the fifteenth. It is as of yet only the thirteenth. Two days is not such a long time to wait. Perhaps, as he said, he will have some work for us."

Claude Monpelier had been their boss when they were working the supply lines. He had had the job of contracting and locating specialists for many companies in North Africa. Prior to that, the Belgian-born Monpelier had served as sergent chef with the Troisième Battalion Parachutiste des Étrangère. It was from there he knew Langers and Beidemann.

"Well, I hope he comes soon. The way you eat up our money, it won't last much longer."

Gus gulped down half a liter of wine to top off his meal. "Carl, I am surprised at you. You never have any faith in our luck. Something will happen. It always does."

Sourly Langers grunted back, "I know, but when you're around it usually means trouble."

Gus finished his wine, blithely ignoring the slander. Suddenly he rose from his seat, beaming with smugness. "See! I told you he would come. Trust me, I know that he brings our fortune with him. Claude is not one to waste talent such as ours."

Looking over his shoulder in the direction Gus was facing, Carl did indeed see Monpelier coming toward them: sunburned, hair and eyebrows bleached by years in the desert sun to an albino white. He still had the look of the Legion to him, straight back, strong, spare body. His face might have once been handsome, but too many fights had rearranged the bone structure. A once-proud Gallic nose now rested between his cheekbones like a mutilated piece of sausage.

Gus swept him into a chair, gurgling happily, "Welcome, *mon vieux*. What is it you have for us?"

Claude merely gave Gus one of the looks he normally reserved for jackals, vultures, and other vile things that crawled upon the face of the earth. Carl ignored both of them. It was an old and time-honored ritual between them.

"Well first, you great hulking beast, can you not see that I am faint from lack of wine?"

"*Good idea*!" Gus roared out loud enough that the snakes living in the ruins of nearby Carthage could hear. "Wine, do you hear? Wine for the troops. We've been raping and ravaging all day and we thirst." He collared a terrified waiter with a fez on his curly head and barked, "Bring wine, and while you're at it water my mule." The waiter started to ask the effendi, or master, where his mule was, but a playful slap on his shoulder sent him reeling toward the kitchen.

Claude sighed wearily and cast a doleful look at Langers. "Can't you put a leash or at least a muzzle on this foul creature?"

Langers smiled for the first time. "No, but I give you permission to do so if you want to try."

Claude knew he was being outmaneuvered and as any wise, old soldier would do, he ignored the remarks completely and got straight to business once he was certain that the other tables were not listening in.

"If you can lower your voices to a normal level, we will get on with what I wish to speak to you about, my friends," he said.

The timid approach of the waiter bearing a liter of the Algerian wine gave them a moment's pause before Claude continued, leaving Gus to pour for them. Gus had no real interest in the details of the job at this point. If Langers liked it, then they would do it, so why bother himself with superfluous dialogue? He was, after all, a most practical man.

Sipping his wine after first testing the bouquet, Claude began.

"Am I not correct in saying that before I had the dubious honor of serving with you, you and your animal here were stationed for a time out of Fort Lapperrine in the Ahaggar Mountains, and from there went on several raids into the territory of the Azbine Tuaregs, the Berber Moslems who inhabit the land between the Talak Air Plains and the Tenere Desert?"

Carl nodded. "Yes, we spent some time there. Bad country, hard people. Why?"

"Well, my friends," he touched his forefinger to the side of his nose to indicate a matter of great confidence, "I have an acquaintance in need of men who know the area and are not afraid to take a small risk." That worried Carl a bit. When Claude referred to anything as a "small risk," he meant the equivalent of trying to mount a bayonet attack across quicksand with sixty-pound packs on your back.

"Just what is this small risk, Sergent Chef?" Carl automatically went back into addressing Monpelier by his old rank.

"You know that since we were 'invited' to leave Algeria, there have been many troubles. One of them has to do with a chieftain of the Azbini. He is trying to form an alliance with the other Tuareg tribes, the Allimideni, Ifora, Azjeri, and Ahaggerni, and even those of the Bedouin. He wishes to form an autonomous state of their own. You and I know this will not happen, but it takes only a few fanatics to cause great trouble. And the trouble is this.'' He paused to refresh his palate. ''One of the Azbine chieftains who calls himself Sunni Ali has captives. The son of a rich man and the son's wife, an American girl. They are being held for ransom.''

Langers took a drink of his own wine. This was beginning to get interesting. ''What do they want, money?''

Claude shook his head. ''No, my old one. The son's father is an arms manufacturer. They want weapons, many weapons: machine guns, mortars, anti-aircraft guns. But the father cannot supply them. His government has found out about the ransom and will not permit the exchange for as you know, it does not take much to start a guerrilla war and keep it going for some years with a few thousand modern rifles and machine guns.

''So, as he cannot give them what they ask for, he has come to me to find men who will attempt a rescue. That is all. You just go in, get the boy and his wife, and bring them out. *Très* simple, *n'est-ce pas?*''

''*That's all!* You know that country. It's hell out there. How do we get in and how do we get out? There's nothing but thousands of miles of nothing out there!''

Claude affected a wounded look. "Ah, but that is why the father will pay so well. However, if you feel it is beyond your talents and do not have the need for twenty-five thousand American dollars, I will go elsewhere, eh?" he said, shrugging his shoulders matter-of-factly.

Carl pushed him back down in his chair. "Knock the crap off, Claude. We're interested, but we need to know more before making a decision."

Monpelier knew he had them or he would not have been stopped from leaving. "Very well. This is what I can tell you now. Our weaponsmaker is a very rich man, and while he cannot get guns to trade for his son, he can supply you with whatever else you may require in terms of equipment. Airplanes, vehicles, communications equipment. His government knows what we wish to try and they have no objection to it. As long as the Tuaregs receive no weapons, we can do as we wish in the matter."

"You did say we, didn't you, Claude? Are you going in with us?"

Claude hid behind his wine glass. "Alas, no, my friends, I am afraid that I have other duties which will prevent me from accompanying you on this minor excursion. I do wish that I could attend the festivities. I know you and your creature. I am confident the desert will never be the same after you two leave."

Gus ordered two more bottles of wine, making

certain the waiter knew to put them on Claude's bill.

Langers went back to the subject. "Okay! The price is all right for me and Gus but there'll be other expenses, and we may have to hire a few more men. In fact, I know we will."

"I have anticipated your needs, my friends. And if we have, as the Americans say, 'a deal,' I will leave you with advance funds now so that you may begin to plan the operation. But know that it must be done quickly. The Tuaregs can be stalled in the matter for only a short time. Then they will do horrible things to the boy and worse to the girl. Remember Medea?"

Langers remembered. There had been great evil done there, torture and slaughter on both sides that would have left the Nazi Gestapo in awe. "All right, how much time do we have?"

"Two, perhaps three weeks. No more."

Sitting silently Langers tried to recall all he could of the terrain between the Talak and the Tenere. None of it was good. "I need more information," he said. "Do you have any idea of just where they are being held and by how many tribesmen?"

Claude gave Gus another dirty look as the second order for two more liters of wine was given to the waiter, before replying, "Yes, of course we have some information and I hope to acquire more in a few days. For now concern yourself with transport and finding the other men you will require—I may be able to help you there. Also, the chieftain who has the prisoners has at best three hundred men, but probably less than half will be with him as the others will be needed to tend their flocks. So you will have to deal with perhaps only one to two hundred Tuaregs.''

Carl groaned. One to two hundred of some of the meanest and toughest men the desert had ever spawned. Speculating more to himself than to anyone else, he mumbled, ''I'll give odds that they're holed up on Mt. Baguezane northeast of Agadez.''

Claude nodded in agreement. ''You are probably correct. But it is not such a great mountain; it only rises to about six thousand feet. As I said, I have some more information coming. It should give us the exact location where they are being held. There cannot be too many places up there with enough water to sustain them. So we will find them.

''Have confidence in me. I will contact you again in two days, three at the most. By this time you will have considered the worst possible conditions and will be able to give me your requirements in men and material.''

This was going to be a bit rough. But if it went down right the money was good for a few days' work. What was the name Claude had called the Azbine chief? Sunni Ali? To Claude he asked, ''Sunni Ali? Wasn't that the name of the king of the old Songhai Empire in the fifteenth century?''

Claude rose, leaving a stuffed envelope on the table. "But of course it was. I am so glad to see that you, unlike your pet ape, are not a complete illiterate. It makes me feel so much more reassured that I have been correct, as I always am, in my decisions. I will see you here at the same time in two or three days, no more. If I do not appear, then the money in the envelope is yours. *Au revoir, mes amis.*"

"Yeah. Good-bye, Claude."

Monpelier was headed for the door when Gus yelled to the waiter, "Be sure to collect for the wine from the little shit before he gets away."

Claude Monpelier shrugged his shoulders as only the French can do and paid the waiter. He left the cafe murmuring the word *merde* over and over.

CHAPTER TWO

Leaving the cafe they wandered back into the streets. They were laid with cobblestones hundreds of years old, many taken from buildings that had seen the coming and the passing of Crusaders. The faces that watched the backs of the two feringi, as the foreigners were disdainfully referred to, could have belonged to that distant time.

In the envelope was enough money, a mixture of enough dinars and American dollars, to last them for a week or two, or to buy passage to another place if the deal with Monpelier didn't work out. Either way they were better off than they were before. But there was one thing about Monpelier: he didn't pass out money unless he wanted you committed. As far as Carl was concerned, this job was a go.

A change of residence to a hotel which had telephone service and showers was their first move. Tunis was baking beneath the hammer of the North African sun. It was near the midday hour and, as in all hot climes, activity slowed down. Those that could found shade to take naps or ate slow lunches and sipped sweet mint tea served from brass pots. Carl and Gus took the opportunity to avail themselves of the hotel's shower. There was no hot water but it didn't matter. The water temperature was warmer than blood, anyway, yet it still cooled the skin.

Gus settled on his single bed by the window where he could catch what little breeze existed. Carl lay back on his bed, naked save for shorts, his eyes closed as he felt the moisture left on his skin from his shower evaporate. Soon it would be gone, then his own body fluids would replace the water from the shower.

A horrible rasping, gurgling noise broke through the hum of flies swarming outside the screened window. Gus was snoring. Squeezing his eyes tightly shut, Langers thought for a moment about strangling the sleeping giant, but the desire passed quickly. It was much too warm to keep such hostile thoughts for very long. It simply required too much effort. Besides which, Gus did have some good qualities. One day, Langers promised himself when he had time he would take a few hours and try to think of one.

Outside he heard the plaintive cry of an Arab water vendor wandering the narrow streets, filling the cups of the thirsty with water he promised was as pure as the tears of a virgin, but smelled like the bladder of a dead camel. He rolled over to get on a dry spot. Beneath him the thin cover was already soaked with his sweat.

Gods! It had been a long time since he and Gus had frozen on the steppes of Russia. There had been the ice and the snow winds that peeled frostbitten skin from the face and froze the delicate tissue in the lungs. He almost wished they were back. No! That was a lie. There was no way he could ever wish for that time to return. The Twenty-sixth Panzer Regiment. He and Gustaf Beidemann were the last survivors of their tank crew. All the others were long dead, left on the frozen fields of Mother Russia along with hundreds of thousands of others who had fought and died—for what? An ideology of some sort.

Memories overcame the present. Once more Langers smelled diesel fumes and cordite, heard the rasping rumble of tank treads as they crashed into each other during the Battle of Kursk. There the smoke of battle was so thick, tanks couldn't see each other at a distance of thirty meters and a hundred thousand men a day were killed or wounded. Kursk! The Dnieper River Line! Red Guards, SS, Kalmuks, and partisans. Trains filled with munitions and living cargo that was to be taken to extermination centers. German soldiers with shell casings hammered into the backs of their necks or left crucified on battlefields. On both sides such an incredible madness.

Mind half-awake, half-numb he dreamed. Faces passed before and around him, hundreds of dead men. Storms of lightning, caused by thousands of heavy guns, crashed, ripping open the earth to receive the dead. Faces, faces . . .

His eyes jerked open. He couldn't take anymore. Through his nightmare Gus had slept the sleep of a child. He was the only true innocent Carl had ever known. Nothing bothered him. His memories of pain were short, therefore he could sleep when others cried out in the night.

Carl slept no more, afraid of what might come. It was easier to just put his mind at a distance and wait for the sun to begin its decline. When the shadows at last grew longer, he rose and showered again, changed into his cleanest dirty shirt, and shook Gus back into the real world.

"C'mon, let's go out for a while, maybe get something to drink or eat."

"Eat! Drink! Be right with you, comrade."

By the time they hit the streets the temperature had dropped into the nineties, almost comfortable. There were people everywhere: Arabs, vendors, women with the veil and without, children running in packs among stalls, wilted Europeans with red, sweaty eyes. One and all seemed to be on the streets now that the worst heat of the day had passed. Near the bazaar they stopped for Gus to refuel. Spiced meats and wine once more disappeared down his maw.

"Let's go over to the Club Chat Rose. I want to see if there's anyone around we might be able to use," Carl said.

Gus took the lead, cutting through the throngs; he was a human battering ram that ignored all in its path. Dirty looks and curses describing his parentage for ten generations slipped off of him. But no one stood in his path. Leaving a wake behind him of frustrated, angry people, they passed the street of coppersmiths, cut over near the old mosque where muezzins still called the faithful to prayer, made a sharp left by the dyers' streets, walked three more blocks, and they were there.

It was the good time, too. The sun was near setting and the streets were growing darker with the creeping shadows, which at dusk took over the city. Vendors were taking down their stalls, closing till the rise of the new sun, but other shops were just preparing to open. It was shift change in Tunis.

The Chat Rose, or Pink Pussy, as Gus liked to call it, was one of the watering holes for the leftovers of a dozen nations. The smell of alcohol drove Gus through the door first. Carl let him go. It was never wise to get in front of Gus when he was after food, booze, or pussy. One might get trampled, unintentionally of course, but the painful end result would be the same.

Gus cast his eyes over the motley crew which the Chat Rose catered to. A few limeys, several Germans, a couple of Polish sailors without good sense to stay closer to the harbor. And in the corner sipping Pernod quietly, his hands holding the small glass between them, was the one they sought.

"Dominic!"

At Gus's greeting several of the customers started to dive under their tables looking for cover, mistaking the explosion of sorts for a mortar attack.

Dominic showed no response; it was a salutation he was long used to.

Slowly raising his eyes from the table he looked up to see the dark hulk of Gus coming toward him, followed by a shorter but not much less squarer form.

"*Ciao*, Gus, Carl. What brings you to the asshole of the world?"

Gus took Dominic Ciardello's glass from him, tossed the remains down neatly, made a face, and ordered a bottle of scotch to be brought to the table. Carl sat on his left, Gus on his right, letting their chairs face the door and inner room.

Carl worried about Dominic. His face, though still handsome, was drawn. Thick black, curly hair cut short framed his old-young face. His body was slight, almost boyish, but very strong and quick. Carl knew his ailment. He had fallen victim to the sickness called killing. Since Dien Bien Phu and then Algeria he had seen the sickness eat up the Italian. Dominic knew it, too. He was not stupid and the need to kill made him sick of himself. He knew what his problem was but had no way to resist it.

The bottle was brought by a tavern wench of mixed ancestry. For centuries Tunis had been a stopping place for every ship that plied the

Mediterranean. The girl was only the long-term genetic result of such visits. Deftly she avoided Gus's paws as she placed the bottle on the table with three semi-clean tumblers and a pitcher of water. She stood back out of range till Carl paid her and then quickly put distance between her and the beast-man.

Carl did the honors, pouring drinks all around, leaving the others to add water if they pleased.

"How is it for you, Dominic?"

The Italian sipped his whiskey slowly between fingers which held only a trace of tremble to them.

"It goes the same, my friends, but it doesn't matter. Like you two, I wait."

Carl nodded in understanding. "Well, perhaps the waiting is about over. You remember Sergent Chef Monpelier?"

Not waiting for Dominic to answer—he already knew they had met—he continued, "He says he has work for us. Do you wish to hear what the job is?"

Dominic shook his head. "It makes no difference. If you have accepted then I do too." The response was not unusual. They had fought many times side by side.

His eyes showed their first spark of life. He needed to get back into the field again. He could have taken many jobs as an assassin. There was much work of that kind to be had, but he hadn't taken any of it. He still had some of his pride left. He was not a murderer, only one who enjoyed the kill, if a bit excessively.

For a few minutes they sat quietly. Even Gus seemed to slow down a bit as they worked their way through the bottle of whiskey. With the true dark of night on the streets, the Chat Rose began to slowly fill with ex-soldiers, mercenaries, dealers in opium, heroin, and slaves, and with smugglers and thieves.

The lights were turned on to provide what feeble illumination forty-watt bulbs could give. From a phonograph behind the bar the girls played records that somehow all sounded the same whether French, Italian, or American. Among the clientele were a few Arabs with their robes covering expensive suits made in Paris or Rome. Being good Moslems they did not drink the whiskey or wine, leaving that to the men they bargained with, men with hot, hungry looks in their eyes.

Carl knew some of them and knew what they did. Sitting with a man wearing the striped robes of a Berber, though the mixed blood in his face showed he was not, was Alexis Sulman, a specialist in the selling of flesh, usually that of young girls, none older than fourteen, for the brothels in Marseille or Hamburg. He had once approached Carl about working for him. Now when he saw the scar-faced man's eyes on him he felt his stomach nearly turn over. The ex-legionnaire's response to his proposition had been somewhat less than friendly; Sulman had not been able to enjoy sampling any of his stock for several weeks.

Gus saw where Carl was looking and spat on the floor. "Now, there is one who needs to be removed from this vale of tears. I have no argument with honest whores who are old enough to make up their own minds, but that swine sells children. One of these days I think I'll kill him."

Neither Carl nor Dominic commented; it was unnecessary. Since it had been said, it was now only a matter of when Sulman would die. Gus used his chunky forefinger to point straight at Sulman's face. Closing one eye, he sighted over it and whispered *bang!* loud enough for the girls in the back of the bar to hear. Sulman left the customer at his table hurriedly, saying they would meet on the morrow in a more civilized environment.

The cafe girls plied their ancient trade among the clientele, approaching all but the table where the hard-looking man sat. The girls knew them and understood this was not a night to disturb them. The men were left alone. The bottle at their table grew empty.

At last, bored with the Chat Rose, Langers left them, handing Dominic a hundred dinars from the roll Monpelier had given him. "You move over to where me and Gus are staying. I'll see you in the morning. Gus, no trouble for now. Behave yourself. I don't want you in jail. If Monpelier comes through, we could move out at anytime. So be good and keep away from Sulman. We can always settle with him later."

Gus affected a pout which didn't work. Mockingly he replied, "Ah! You are a hard master, effendi, but this lowly one hears you and will obey. I shall, in an attempt to gain merit, take this lost child," he nudged Dominic, "into my protection until the morrow."

Langers just shook his head. Gus never changed. Paying the bill, he left them sitting, knowing they would be okay. After all the jokes and bullshit were done with, Gus was reliable where it counted.

Langers wanted to get outside and be alone for a time. The city was too heavy, confining. Letting his feet pick their path, he wandered through the streets filled with the smells that can only be found in a city of the East. Smells of cinnamon and curry, sandlewood and musk mingled with that of industrial chemicals and DDT. Mounds of trash moved as though they had a life of their own from the maggots that bred in them. There was nothing new; he had seen and smelled the same ten thousand times before.

His feet led him at last to the outskirts of the city. The night was clear as only the desert night can be. Moisture from the sea had been pushed back by winds from the desert. Resting his hip on a boulder, Carl looked back to see the way he had come.

He was on a rise outside of the city. In front of him lay the main town and harbor where ship lights rose and fell with the slight movement of the Mediterranean waters. To his back were the rocky hills and mountains, passes and gorges. In those hills and beyond lived, by Western standards, barbarian tribes, Berbers, and some members of the Tuareg tribe if you went far enough. In those same passes lay the bones of Romans and Carthaginians, Vandals and Byzantines, Americans, English, Italians, and Germans. For a dry land it had been well watered over the centuries with blood.

Watching the stars run their eternal course overhead, Carl thought of the land to the south. A harsh, unforgiving land. The job itself sounded simple enough, but few things were ever what they appeared to be. There would be unseen, unknown problems which would end up killing someone. Even that wasn't of any great import. The men they would take with them knew what the odds were.

A breeze from the hills rolled over him. It was good. There would not be many cool breezes when they passed over the mountains. Until they came out, by day it would be an oven designed by a shaitan, an evil spirit, to bake the souls of men in their own shells and by night almost freezing.

CHAPTER THREE

It was with dawn that Carl returned. He had needed the night in the desert to think and feel. Dominic had done as he'd asked and had gone with Gus to their hotel. He was sleeping in Carl's bed, no great surprise. Gus had opened one red eye when he'd come in and been told to go back to sleep, an order promptly obeyed.

After taking a quick shower, Carl went out to breakfast. Until it was time for him to go to the waterfront cafe he just walked. The sounds of the city washed over him: crying children, beggars, muezzins calling out from their minarets for the faithful to come to morning prayer. He moved aside to make room for a group of Coptic priests with tangled beards walking in orderly squads, swinging censers of incense on their way to some place or other.

The appointed time found Langers at the same table as he'd been at the previous day with Gus. Monpelier was relieved to find him sitting alone. Gus always made things so difficult.

"I am glad to see that you are on time, my

friend. It is good. Fortunately, I have been most productive and have most of the information we require, but more will be coming shortly.'' Carl nodded for him to continue.

"It's as we thought. Sunni Ali has made his camp at Mt. Baguezane. The last word is that the boy and girl are well. At his camp he has only perhaps forty armed men full time. The others are with the animals or their families, but they can be summoned within an hour or two. At the massif Ali uses some of the large caves for his stronghold. They control three or four spring-fed ponds for their water. The springs usually flow all year. From here to the massif we can go one of two ways: we can drive the whole way or fly to the strip at Fort Laperrine in the Ahaggar Mountains, where I can have transport and supplies waiting. From there it is not far to the Talak Air Plains and stronghold of our friend Sunni Ali and his Azbine tribesmen. Getting out, well, that leaves us with the same problems. By ground or by air?''

They spoke around the attentions of the waiter and passing customers. "What about the other men?'' Carl asked. "If it's as you say, then we are going to need at least nine or ten more. I found Dominic yesterday and will be taking him. Do you have any others in mind that we can get?''

Monpelier removed a folded piece of paper from his pocket. "I have already found ten more. Like you and your friends, they are all former legionnaires or combat-experienced men. I think they will do quite well for our purposes.''

He handed Langers the list and leaned back while it was read. Refolding the paper, Langers handed it back to Monpelier.

''I think you're right. I know a couple of the men on your list; they are good. And if the others are just as good then we should have no problems. Now what about equipment? We'll need a bit of everything just for contingencies.''

Monpelier ordered a coffee and cakes. His stomach was beginning to rumble a bit. ''I can get almost anything you need. Just make up your list. But let us take things in order. What is your first requirement?''

Langers leaned forward. ''More information. I want pictures of the massif, more info on the background and history of Sunni Ali and the time frame we have to work in.

''As for what transport we need, this is the way I think we should approach it at this time. We'll fly into Fort Laperrine, but only to refuel. First we'll send a few of our men on ahead with the vehicles. They'll meet us in the desert as close to Baguezane as we can get without spooking anyone. If we pulled into any of the villages in a group, the Tuaregs would know of it immediately. We'll take all weapons and heavy gear with us on the plane. There are plenty of salt flats out there that can be used as a landing strip. We'll have the advance party select one and notify us by radio which one we are to use.

"Once the advance party gets clear of the Ahaggar Mountains, they shouldn't have any problems getting out to . . . I would say somewhere . . . ," he searched his memory, "to some place between Tarazit and the oasis at Bilma. Dead between them are several places suitable for our purposes. Also, that would put us in back of Mt. Baguezane. We may want to go after the boy and girl that way. Sunni Ali would most probably not expect a rescue to come at him from the Tenere Desert. Get me all the photos you can on the area and just what section of the mountain he is keeping his camp in. That might change a few things as far as equipment is concerned."

Monpelier agreed. He gave the impression that he had just started putting things together in the last couple of days when, in truth, he had been on the job for the last three weeks. And most of that had been spent in gathering intelligence for just such an operation. "Very good, my friend. I will meet you at Ghudamis in three days. At that time I will bring the rest of your team with me. With your agreement I will go ahead and arrange for air transport to be waiting to take us to Fort Laperrine."

Carl agreed, glad that they wouldn't have to make the 2,000-kilometer drive out there.

Taking another envelope from his jacket pocket, Monpelier handed it across the table. "In here are what salient facts you may need about the hostages and a profile of Sunni Ali, or at least as much as I was able to find out. The Tuaregs, as you know, are a most secretive people. I wish that I had a photo for you but then, it wouldn't do much good since the Tuaregs nearly always keep their faces covered. But he does wear a distinctive jellaba, the traditional cloak, and has gray-blue eyes much like yours.''

Rising from the table Monpelier said, "Well, that is all I have for now. Three days, then, and I will see you in Ghudamis. Stay at the Hotel Saharienne. You might be able to pick up some more current information as to what conditions prevail among the Tuareg tribes. I know that you did have some contacts among some Berbers and Arabs in that area. Perhaps they will know something.''

Langers rose with him. There was no longer any need to sit there in the heat of the day. ''All right. Three days. And bring more money. We'll need to have it for the unexpected expenses that always arise. And bring me at least ten thousand in gold. The contacts I used to have all had one thing in common, they like the sound of gold better than paper.''

Carl left with Monpelier. Outside the cafe Monpelier handed him a set of keys.

"These are yours. There is a red and white Land Rover at the end of the block. It is fully equipped: extra gas cans, water, some rations, blankets, etc. Just what you need for the trip to Ghudamis. I didn't include any weapons. They come later. I don't want you caught with anything that could give the authorities any reason to detain you. I presume you still have some money left. So I'll leave you here.''

Langers had thought about taking one of the local buses to Ghudamis. It was with relief that he now had an alternate form of transport. Bus travel in North Africa was an experience most would much rather do without.

At the hotel he rounded up Ciardello and Gus. ''Get your things while I pay the bill. We're moving out. Monpelier got back to me in a hurry, so it looks like a go.''

Gus stuffed his few belongings into an over-sized musette bag. Dominic had had his ready to go since the previous night. Neither asked where they were heading till they were settled in the Land Rover and on the way out of Tunis.

Dominic looked around him and then at the mountains in the distance. ''Where are we heading?''

''Ghudamis for now. From there we'll just have to see. Monpelier will join us in three days with the rest of the team.''

Traffic was sparse. There were only a few buses, which were jam-packed with people and animals ranging from goats to chickens. More common were carts pulled by weary donkeys and small, thin-haired horses. Their masters urged them along loaded for the marketplaces with heaps of dead wood gleaned from the mountainside to be used as fuel for cooking fires. The only change Carl could see in the carts from 500 years past was that some of them had on old truck or automobile tires instead of wooden wheels.

They had to take the coastal road through Sfax, then around the Gulf of Gabes to the border of Libya. They were eyed with suspicion as they passed over the border, the numbers of their vehicle carefully noted to be passed on later. Carl had decided to take the route that was the better road, in fact the only road. There were trails they could have taken to intercept the road from Tripoli to Ghudamis, but that could have taken them two or even three days to travel. Ghudamis was on the Tunisian side of the border nestling at the point where Tunisia, Libya, and Algeria joined. He figured that they might as well get it over with as far as passing through the border was concerned. Guards at heavily trafficked sites were not nearly as jumpy as those in the more isolated regions. Once they had the Libyan stamp on their passports, it should help them if they ran into any problems before reaching Ghudamis.

Monpelier had it about right. It would take them two days to reach their destination if they didn't run into any problems, and in this part of the world it was a rare excursion when you did not. At Sabratha they took a trail south to intersect the road from Tripoli. They had passed three military patrols since they'd crossed the frontier. The looks they'd received from the crews made

Carl uneasy. Best to play it safe.

Fifty kilometers on a donkey trail and they picked up the main road. By then night was full on them. Carl and Dominic switched places, leaving Gus in the back to eat on dates and figs they had picked up from a roadside vendor. At the village of Nalut they spent the night, taking the vehicle into an enclosed area that served as a patio for the hostel. Theirs was the only motor vehicle in evidence.

Inside they were greeted profusely by the owner, a man with Arab features. Not unusual, this was one of those places where the Bedouin Arabs' and the Berbers' lands merged. Most of the clientele were Arabs who kept to themselves. They sat in small groups sipping their tea or coffee mixed with cardomon, a spice which Arabs have a great fondness for.

The common room was a spare area with a fireplace at the sound end of one wall for cooking. Raised areas for eating rimmed the room which was lit by coal oil lamps. Electricity was fifty kilometers to the south and would have been too expensive if it had been available.

Carl called the innkeeper over as Gus went to inspect what was cooking on the spit over the coals in the fireplace. Dominic looked around uninterestedly.

"We want one room for all of us," Carl told the innkeeper. "And I would advise against anyone getting too close to our vehicle. It would upset me terribly if anything were wrong with it tomor-row.'' His fingers dug into the muscle running from the neck to the shoulder of the tavern master. ''We do understand each other, do we not?''

''Oh yes, effendi. It is most clearly under-stood. I have great love for the English and the French. All will be well. Please be at ease. I give you my word.''

Carl released the pressure. ''Very well. But if things are not as you say, I will take from you more than your word. Now show me to our room.''

Calling Gus away from the fireplace, they fol-lowed the innkeeper up to the second floor and were shown into a room with two cots and a wash basin, nothing more.

''This is the best in my establishment, good sirs, the very best. But there are three of you. Will you not wish another accommodation?''

Carl pushed him out the door. ''No! This will do.''

Gus looked around and opened the window to let in some air. From their window they could see the Land Rover parked close to the wall. ''Why just one room, Carl?''

''Because, you great ape, we are going to take turns staying with the Land Rover so we know it will be there in the morning. You and Ciardello go and bring our things in. I'm going to hit the rack first, seeing as how I did most of the driving. Dominic, you and Gus settle on who takes first watch in the Land Rover."

Carl was asleep before they made it to the Land
Rover and back with their gear. He opened one
eye when they came back in, then closed it immediately after first looking out the window at the
night. He didn't want to go to sleep with the face
of Gustaf Beidemann as the last thing he saw. It
was just too depressing.

Gus graciously took the job of sleeping in the
Land Rover. After all, he could sleep anywhere as
long as he had a full stomach, and he'd seen to that
by taking half of the goat the innkeeper was preparing for his other six guests with him as a
midnight snack.

Several of the hotel guests had looked with lust
at the Land Rover, knowing its worth. When the
shock absorbers groaned under the weight of Gus
as he climbed in, and was obviously not going to
leave, there were several silent moans of frustration. None would go near the Land Rover this
night, not unless they wanted to use guns and that
would wake the city.

The trio was on the road at dawn, not waiting to
take breakfast. They preferred their own cold rations to the fare of the inn. All ate except Gus,
who slept peacefully until they were another fifty
kilometers along the way. The wet regions of the
coast had long since been left behind.

They were now in the Sahara Desert, climbing
over ranges of brown rocks which had been
shaped by the millennia of winds, heat, and cold.

Harsh and foreboding, the Sahara welcomed no one and only those as harsh as it had any chance of surviving in it. Between stone monoliths they drove on. Sunglasses helped to cut the glare but their eyes still turned red and gritty from the strain. Twice they had to stop to shove boulders out of the road.

At midday they pulled over to seek the shade of a rock wall. The Land Rover needed the rest, too. The surface temperature of the sand was over 130 degrees and they had hundreds of miles to go yet before they reached the worst of it.

Each of them tried to take what rest they could from the heat. For four hours they didn't move, not until the sun had long since passed overhead and the earth had had a slight chance to cool.

They wouldn't make it to Ghudamis until long after dark, and that was all right with them. They would take the cold of the desert over the heat.

Somewhat rested, Carl took the wheel again, navigating over a road that had seen little traffic and even less maintenance. But it was the only road to Ghudamis.

In the light of the Land Rover's headlamps, animals which came out at night to hunt crossed the road, eyes bright and glowing but blinded by the glare. There were desert jackals, large-eared foxes, and striped hyenas. All came out in the night to compete for food.

Unseen to the west and south, the dunes waited, stretching for hundreds of miles. The Sahara itself was three and a half million square miles of hell. Carl thought those dimensions would fit Hades perfectly.

Shoulders cramped, muscles burning from the tedious drive, it was with relief that they at last saw dim lights glowing in a few brown mud-brick houses. They were coming into Ghudamis. It was about time. In the last hour the temperature had dropped to thirty-five degrees from the day's peak of 108. The Sahara did not have cloud cover enough to retain any of the heat of the day.

Gus pointed to a grove of trees outside of the village. "Isn't that where the Hotel Saharienne is?"

"I think so," Carl said. "We'll find out in a few minutes." Pulling into a palm-lined driveway which led up to a three-story stuccoed building, they came to a halt gratefully.

The passenger door of the Land Rover was opened by a smiling black man wearing a gold-trimmed red jacket and a fez. Despite their road-filthy and dust-encrusted appearance, he greeted them as if they were visiting royalty. Upon the clap of his hands, porters appeared out of the dark to carry their gear into the lobby, which could have come from a Hollywood movie set: potted palms and plants, rotating overhead fans, furniture which belonged in the attics and cellars of a hundred years ago.

The Saharienne had once been somebody's dream, built by an Englishman who'd thought that when oil was found, Ghudamis would become a major crossroads. It had gone through several hands since then. It was now owned by a Hindu family who kept the *pukka sahib* attitude: patiently they had waited for the flood of tourists and travelers to come for two generations now, and with the calm resignation of the Orient, they were ready to wait two more generations or however long they had to. Meanwhile, they would keep the hotel ready and fully staffed. Of its one hundred rooms, only four were occupied, three of those by a geological survey crew from Belgium and the other by a permanent resident—one of those leftovers from the colonial days who had chosen to stay and die.

"Welcome, sirs. Have you a reservation?"

Carl admitted that they did not. The Hindu clerk gave them a slightly distasteful look through his wire-rimmed glasses, as if to say their parents should have taught them better. He went through the ritual of checking his guest register, then with great satisfaction at being able to squeeze them in, replied aloofly, "Ah, yes, good sirs. You are most fortunate. I see that we will be able to accommodate you. Please sign the register."

They did as they were bade. Even Gus seemed a bit subdued by the clerk, as if he recognized one who had even more fantastic dreams than he did.

Carl gave the car keys to a porter. They were requested to please wait a moment. The clerk vanished to the rear office. A few seconds passed.

Then they heard a coughing that changed to a steady chug and lights came on in the lobby, electric lights from overhead chandeliers. For some reason it made the place seem even more odd than it was when lit only by lamps and candles.

Proudly the desk clerk announced, "You may go to your rooms now, good sirs, and have a pleasant stay at the Hotel Saharienne."

A red-fezzed bellboy took them to a lift, making a ceremony out of turning the bronze handle forward till power gave the winch enough strength to lift the cage up to the first floor, where they were shown to two rooms. Carl had put Gus with Dominic, thinking that it was best that neither of them were left alone too long. Besides, he needed some space to himself to think for a time. The rooms were like the lobby. A touch of old England seventy years ago. After accepting his gratuity, the bellboy announced that the electricity would be turned off upon his return to the lobby but every evening at dinner it was turned on again for two hours.

The shower was hot. On the roof was a holding tank painted black to absorb the heat of the already searing sun. Water came nearly steaming from the pipes. The only good thing about hot showers in tropical climates was that it felt cool for a few minutes after you got out.

A light meal of boiled eggs and toast served with English tea and marmalade started the day off fairly well. Gus had four orders.

Looking at Dominic over his cup, Langers was concerned about him. Since they'd gone on the road Langers had been keeping a watch on Dominic. He seemed a bit more at ease. Gus was always the same; he hadn't changed since the first day they'd met in Russia. Seven long years of fighting together and the only time he'd ever seen him down was when young Manny Ertl died in the winter of '44 on the Dnieper River Line. He'd lost track of Gus during the retreat from Russia and found him again in the Legion, where thousands of former members of the Wehrmacht ended up after the war was over. France had needed trained soldiers to fight her wars in Indochina and she found many of them in the defeated armies of her former enemy.

Langers shook the past off again. They had things to do today.

CHAPTER FOUR

Carl had Gus and Dominic service the Land Rover. They used their spare gear and went about replacing the air and oil filters. While they did this Langers took the time to go over the report Monpelier had given him.

Inside the envelope were pictures of the two hostages. For the first time he had names: Jason St. Johns and his bride, Jeannine. There was a striking resemblance between them. Both were in their early twenties. From the black and white photos he guessed they both had dishwater blond or sun-bleached hair. A good-looking couple, intelligent faces. Both were well educated, she at schools in Switzerland and France, he at Yale. It appeared that Sunni Ali had picked them up while they were on their honeymoon taking a motor safari across Africa. The boy's father was Andrew St. Johns, an international arms broker who had mega-dollars and only one heir.

As for Sunni Ali, there was nothing new. He was still a mystery. He had just appeared among the tribes one day and had risen to leader of the

Azbnei Tuaregs—all this in the last two years.
The only known fact about him was that he always
did what he said he would do. If he said he'd kill
the hostages, then that was exactly what would
take place. It was known that he spoke French and
English fluently, as well as Arabic and Tamahag,
the Tuareg dialect.

The rest of the envelope contained pictures of
the Mt. Baguezane region. All of them were aerial
views, some of which had been torn out of old
magazines. That was okay; nothing there would
change very much in just a few years.

That was it. Not much! He'd have to do like
Monpelier had suggested and try to contact some
of those he had dealt with during the troublesome
past. The one man he needed in particular was
Sharif Mamud ibn-Hassani, an old desert fox
who was the master of Wadi Jebel, only a few
hours drive from Ghudamis. He'd make inquiries.
If the sharif was still alive, he would go and see
him. During the Algerian operation, Sharif
Mamud had supplied him with information about
the rebel terrorists. As often as the French Colonials had been attacked by them, so had his
people, the Bedouin Arabs. Sharif Mamud had
explained his informing by saying that if he was
going to be conquered, he would prefer it to be by
people who at least knew how to cook.

Returning to the hotel, Carl found Gus on the
porch sipping iced lemonade. ''Looks good,
Gus.'' He ordered one from the attending waiter,

who stood waiting politely just out of earshot. When it was brought to him, before drinking it he placed the glass between his eyes. The cold almost hurt. He ran it over the outside of his face. The chill was delicious. Only then did he drink, taking half the glass in one long swallow.

Gus smiled with approval. "Good shit, huh? Comes from their own groves."

"Yes, it's good. Now listen, if he's still around we're going over to see old Sharif Mamud tomorrow."

Gus nodded. "I wondered if we'd see the old goat thief while we were in the area. If anyone knows anything it'll be him. An information service, that's what he is, a regular encyclopedia."

Looking around, Langers asked, "Where's Dominic at?"

Gus pointed his glass to the road. "In the village taking a look around. He should be back soon."

"The Land Rover?"

"Everything's in order. It's watered and gassed and the spare cans have been refilled. We're ready to go."

Carl grunted "Good" as he drained the last of his glass. The waiter approached him bearing a slip of paper on a silver salver, saying, "Master Langers, sir. This is for you." Carl took the note and gave the man what must have been his first tip in weeks.

After reading it, he put the paper in his pocket.

"Monpelier will be here tomorrow night. I want you to go and find Dominic, then check around to see if Sharif Mamud is at the Wadi Jebel. No sense making the trip if he's dead."

With resignation for an unpleasant task, Gus hauled his carcass from the comfortable chair.

"*Zu Befehl,* Herr Feldwebel." He gave a mock salute. "Yes, sir, Herr Sergeant."

Carl ignored him.

He watched Gus's back as he trundled off toward the sun-baked bricks of the village, then went back inside to wait. He knew that if Sharif Mamud was still alive Gus would find out. Not many could refuse him. Just his imposing size started most tongues wagging freely.

Dominic came back in and joined him, placing his thin frame gratefully on the cushions. He wiped perspiration from his face and the back of his neck. "I forgot how damned hot it was out here, and we're not anywhere near the bad part yet." Snapping his fingers he ordered lemonade. "Gus told me about you wanting to go and see the old sharif. Good idea. Which of us is going to stay here and wait for Monpelier?"

Carl didn't have to think about it very much. Gus drove Monpelier crazy, and he and Dominic knew it. "It would probably be better if you were here, Dominic. You know how Gus gets under Monpelier's skin."

Dominic gave one of his rare smiles. "Gus could get under the skin of a rhino. It's all right with me. I have no love for riding in that machine any more than I have to. You two go and have the fun. I'll hold things down here till you get back."

It was nearly dark before Gus returned. "The old goat's still at Wadi Jebel," he reported. "Now let's go and get something to eat before I faint from hunger."

Neither Carl nor Dominic felt any sympathy for Gus's hunger. Grease stains on his shirt told the story of why it had taken him so long to get back. The beast had been feeding again.

From Ghudamis they cut over to the east, taking the road to Messouda on the Algerian side of the border. At a checkpoint Carl and Gus showed their papers to bored guards who were more interested in the two cartons of American cigarettes they had impounded than they were in the two men in the Land Rover.

Dropping down off the mountain, they could see the sun-baked brick wall of the town in the distance. Small patches of green dotted the countryside, patches where vegetation had taken root. Here rain from the mountains fell to the basin, gathering in underwater reservoirs formed in the past millenia.

Three kilometers from Messouda they turned back to the northwest, driving on a narrow rutted trail till they saw what they had come for, the oasis of Wadi Jebel.

●   ●   ●

"Welcome and may Allah protect you. Share my tent and salt. Be welcome."

Sharif Mamud gave his guests greetings in the traditional manner of his race. Instinctively he knew that their visit meant silver or gold for his purse. He had dealt with the scarface in the past. He trusted him to live up to any agreement they came to. This foreigner was an honorable man—if somewhat disconcerting. He knew not where the name for him originated, but from his personal knowledge it was accurate. Al-Kattel . . . the killer.

During the troubles the Legion had many hard men but no one who struck so much fear into the hearts of enemies as had this gray-eyed one. Sharif Mamud knew that he had been one who never failed when sent to kill. Ah! That had been a bloody time. And profitable for one who was not bothered by such things as national loyalty or political passions. It was Sharif Mamud who had been the eyes and ears of al-Kattel and upon payment, the voice. And now he had returned with the big ugly one who stood as the mountain had stood before the prophet Mohammed. The one whose name sounded like the gurgling of the stomach of a camel in heat. Gu*ss*. A most ugly sound yet it suited the bearer well.

The sides of the tent were raised, closed flaps invited unwelcome listeners. Sharif Mamud waved away a bothersome fly with a horsetail whisk. "It has been a long time, effendi, since these eyes have seen you and your so large shadow.''

Carl sat on cushions, face-to-face with Sharif Mamud. Gus kept an eye on the outside. Waiting till tea had been brought and the server departed, Carl finally said, ''I have need of your long nose and sharp ears, my friend.''

Sharif Mamud nearly glowed. He was right, there would be gold. Restraining his excitement he responded with calculated disinterest. ''Ah, but what may this old one know that would be of interest to one such as yourself? There is no longer any war. The lands are quiet, the tribes are at peace, the French are gone. What could it be that you wish to know?''

Sipping the tea with sucking sounds to show his appreciation, Carl waded through Sharif Mamud's ritual foreplay. ''True, Sharif, things are different and the land is quiet. But that may change soon. There is trouble coming from the south.''

''Not from my people surely, al-Kattel—'' The title slipped out. Sharif Mamud recovered quickly. ''—Effendi.''

Carl waved it away. ''That does not matter. I do not take offense. In my years I have been called much worse. But let us keep that name between us; it's not for outside ears.''

Sharif Mamud bowed his head slightly, the folds of his turban framing his face. ''As you wish. Now back to how I may be of service. What is this trouble you speak of?''

"Sunni Ali of the Azbnei Tuaregs.''

Sharif Mamud sucked the back of his teeth. *"Aiii!* I presume you do not mean the Sunni Ali of old but the new one.''

Carl nodded. "Of course. Tell me what you know of him.''

Sharif Mamud poured more tea, giving himself time to collect his thoughts and calculate how much to give away for free.

"It is said, by whom I do not know, but it is said that this new Sunni Ali would be a torch in the night. He is a man without vice or tolerance. A most hard and unforgiving person trapped in the sands of yesteryear, to which he wishes a return.''

Sharif Mamud paused. Significantly his right hand lay palm open, casually, on the inlaid table. Carl smiled. His own hand was already filled. Over Sharif Mamud's palm he let loose a stream of gold coins until the palm was filled, then he said, "My old friend, even I know that words must be given nourishment that they might ripen into truth and wisdom.''

Mamud knew within a centime exactly how much had been put into his palm by the weight of it. It was enough.

"It is good to speak with one who has not blinded himself with philosophies or dreams. Reality can be so much more rewarding.'' The coins disappeared into the folds of his jellaba.

"More tea, al-Kattel?" Carl accepted with grace, and waited.

Picking up where he had left off Sharif continued, "As I said, my friend, this Sunni Ali is a most strange man, and it has been whispered by a few that he is not of the Azbini or even of the Tuareg. But no one knows from whence he came. One day he was there, that is all that is known. He has taken for his own many young men from different tribes including my own."

Leaning closer he hissed, "It is good that you have come. Too long have these lands been watered with blood and tears. This Sunni Ali is evil. If perchance you happen to meet him, gain favor with Allah and kill him without hesitation or conscience. I take your gold for such is my weakness of spirit, but I would have told you without payment, such is my distaste for the veiled man."

Carl knew what he meant. Those bad years were still fresh to the memory. That they would come again he never doubted, but they didn't have to come so soon.

"You said that perhaps he is not of the Azbini. Then what is he? You have sharp ears, old one. Have there not been rumors of his origin?"

Mamud scratched at his beard. "Rumors, yes. Some have said that he is one of those desert-loving *Englesi* who has gone mad and become more Arab than the Arab, more Berber than the Berber, and more Tuareg than the Tuareg. Others claim he is a legionnaire who, when he deserted, was taken in by the Tuaregs, for he speaks several languages, something most unusual for a Tuareg. There are many stories. Take your choice of them. One will serve as well as another.

"One other thing I know is of the guests he keeps at his camp by the mountain known as Baguezane. If my feeble mind has not completely lost its ability to do simple mathematics, I would conclude that they are the reason you are asking these questions. Is it not so?"

"Yes, that is correct, you desert jackal. It has fallen to me and those under me to take the two, as you called them, 'guests' from the hospitality of Sunni Ali."

Sharif Mamud rose from his cushions. "Come with me. We shall walk and talk during this the most pleasant time of the day when the sun gives way to the night and the air is cool."

Gus started to trail after them but was detoured by Mamud. "No, my large one. Remain and dine. Lamb roasted with mint jelly and grape leaves and sweet rice is being brought to you now. Stay and do that which you do best, and leave thinking to those who are the thinkers. Feed, thou offspring of an elephant, feed."

Gus would have been indignant but the mention of lamb roasted with mint jelly was too much, especially as the platters were at that moment being brought to him by the women of Sharif Mamud's household. The aroma removed any thought of insult or retaliation from his thick brow. Carl smiled at him as a parent would smile at a slow but well-loved child.

Mamud led the way between rows of date palms to the edge of the oasis where they climbed to a rocky ridge and sat upon the stones. These craggy ridges, on the horizon beyond the Sahara, kept the moisture of the sea from being dissipated by the desert, giving life to a thin green strip along the North African coast.

The day was giving way reluctantly as the shadows grew longer and darker across the land. Mamud looked to the south, his eyes going beyond the mountains. "It is hard out there, my friend. There is a saying which has much truth to it. And that is: if you cross the Sahara, to stay on the trail look for the bones of those who have died. They mark the trail. When you cannot find them, you are truly and forever lost."

Carl knew that even though the danger that he spoke of was real, in the deep caverns of his soul Mamud still longed for the freedom he had known of the desert before he became master of Wadi Jebel. Out there in the great silence was the only true freedom for one such as he.

"Al-Kattel, I will go with you in your quest. If you will cross the Baguezane, you will have need of one who knows the way. Once, when I was young, my sire pitched our tents at the base of the mountain. My boyhood friends and I spent many months learning its secrets. I know how to get to

the camp of Sunni Ali. You must come from the
east over the mountain. No one will look for you
to come out of the desert.''

Mamud was not a young man but Carl knew
that he had hidden reserves of strength. And he
was right, he would be needed. Perhaps he would
even make the difference. ''Very well,
graybeard. If you would go once more into the
desert, then come with us as friend and companion.''

Mamud faced toward the mountains, now only
a faint, soon to be invisible line against the rim of
heaven. ''Good. It is right that I go with you. I
have been too long away. The soft life has taken
much from me, and now I have little left to give.
My days grow short and I am not needed as I once
was. My sons have sons. They are not of the
desert anymore. Soon they will want cars and
planes, vacations in Europe. That is well enough
for them, but I wish to return one more time to the
furnace that once made my people great in the
eyes of God.''

Turning his eyes to Carl he breathed deeply,
''Ah, yes I know. I ramble too much. Dream too
much. But you know that when only the stars
separate one from the face of God, when the
djinns, the spirits, ride the winds and great dunes
move as oceans over the land, it is easy to dream.
To dream of those years past when my people rode
out of the furnace as hard as steel, pure of mind
and eye. With the sword and the Koran they
cleansed the earth.''

Carl thought he saw a tear in Mamud's eye. "And then, my friend?"

Mamud looked toward the north. "Then we fell from favor and became like those we conquered. The cities took us and with the taking we were corrupted in the eyes of Allah, may His name be praised. For this did he turn his favor from us, and now for such a long time we have been a small people who fight among ourselves and accomplish nothing. We have little left and that is one reason why I wish to go with you. This Sunni Ali must be stopped. The ways of old are not to be brought back. The world is too different. All that he would accomplish would be to speed up the dying. I would have the old ways die like myself, with time and as much grace as possible."

Carl understood all too well. Casca Rufio Longinus had seen nations rise and fall, men and religions grow old and unneeded. He shook the thoughts from him. Casca alias Carl Langers was to live in this time. Yet if he could have he would return to the other time also.

A chill ran over Langers. In only a few minutes the temperature had dropped twenty degrees. "Let's go back now," he said. There is much to do. We will meet again perhaps in one or two days. At that time be ready to go. Also, if you find out anything more about Sunni Ali, contact me immediately."

Mamud led the way back. Carl watched him carefully. His steps were strong, sure, his back still as straight as a *jirad*, a spear. He knew the old man would carry his weight, more than carry it. When one was ready to die as he was, the last reserves of strength from body and soul stood by to be called on. He envied Sharif Mamud his death. For he knew that the hand of Allah had touched the old man. He was ready for paradise. Carl wished him well in the afterlife. *In sha' Allah*, the will of God.

Gus was ready for them. Nothing remained save the bones, which had been well picked, sucked, and smacked over by the fleshy lips of the big German. When they returned, Gus was wandering around outside of Sharif Mamud's tent eating a handful of sweet dates for dessert.

Carl left Sharif Mamud at the door of his tent, telling him "Rest well and dream the dreams of old. For I know that they will come to you again and this time your dream of freedom will be realized, for that is what you seek and what you shall find."

Mamud nodded his head. It was good to speak to one who understood. The scar-faced feringi was more than he seemed. There were depths to the man's soul that were deep, very deep, and in those depths were great sorrows. Mamud wished for him, too, to one day find peace.

"*Salaam aleikum*, my friend." He spoke the parting words.

"*Aleikum salaam*, Sharif Mamud ibn-Hassani. Peace be with you. Till we meet again." To his large friend he said, "Come on, Gus, let's get going. Monpelier should be there by now.''

Gus climbed into the driver's seat and started up the Land Rover. The ride back to the fort seemed much longer. Or perhaps it was just that Carl felt very, very old.

CHAPTER FIVE

He did not like the caves; they choked him with their closeness. Holes in the earth were the domain of the dead. The walls were stained with smoke ten thousand years old and covered in parts with prehistoric paintings. It stank inside of stale death, not of the invigorating purity of the desert.

Guards at the entrance to the caves bowed as he passed, their faces, like his, kept hidden beneath the black indigo-dyed veils. He was their master and they were his dogs to do his bidding. Their only reason for existing was to obey and serve. Sunni Ali felt the same discontent for them: the warriors of the Tuareg had too long been confined. Soon it would be time to set his dogs loose to reclaim their ancient heritage.

Striding across a cleared area between larger-than-man-sized boulders he went to his tent, ignoring the rest of his encampment whose tents had been set to take advantage of what shade was cast by the boulders of the mountain. But his eyes missed nothing. Sentries stood on high points to observe all that passed in front of their eyes, eyes which could see much farther than those of ordinary men, eyes which had been trained in the constant glare of the Saharan sun. His women he had sent away. There was no place for women in the affairs of men. They were a distraction at this time. He would be served only by the men of his tribe.

Resting on cushions of woven horse hair, Sunni Ali crossed his legs and removed his veil. His face was stark, surprisingly pale where the sun had not touched it. The bones of his cheeks were prominent, giving him the gaunt and intense look of a desert falcon. He wished nothing at this time and waved away his attendants. He wanted only to think.

When the weapons came he would gather to him the tribes of the desert and make war. He did not have any illusions about being able to win a major war, but he could make it so expensive for the enemy in terms of life and cost that his people would be granted their freedom. Freedom from artificial boundries, freedom to ride as they had for a thousand years, obeying only the laws of Allah, blessed be His name, and those of the desert. Let the rest of the world do as it wished. Let them destroy themselves in their quest for power. He wanted only that which was theirs and the return of their way of life without interference. If it meant that thousands would die, that too would be in the hands of God.

Once he had possession of the weapons the

boy's father had promised, Sunni Ali would then call a great gathering of the tribes to him. Already he had sent emissaries to the Bedouin and the other Berber. He heard back from them that they would wait and see if he could deliver on his promise. Rifles alone were not enough to fight tanks and airplanes. Courage they had, but too many times in the past they had seen the bravery of their fighting men destroyed by the more modern weapons of the invaders. To wage war they had to know that they had at least a fighting chance. That is all. No one would have believed a guarantee of victory, but a fighting chance was all that was required for them to gather their warriors and once more come out of the desert to drive the invaders and infidels from their lands. Who knew? If they were successful in their first attempt then it might be that the other tribes of the Berbers and even some of the Arabs would come to ride with them and declare a great *jihad*, a holy war.

Sunni Ali saw all this clearly. In the remote regions of his mind there was the thought that perhaps, just perhaps, he could be the flame which would rally all the followers of the prophet together and once and for all rid themselves of the feringi. Then the tribes could go back to settling their differences among themselves as they always had.

Legend and prophecy had forecast the birth of a great one who would rally Islam. It was possible that it could be him. He did have the space between his teeth that the prophets had said would mark the *Mahdi*.

Sunni Ali lost sight of reality in his dreams, dreams he had as a child reborn. He had listened to the storytellers talk of the past when they were free men, of the great warriors who with sword and fire brought the word of Allah to the unbeliever. He believed in dreams. Oft times at night he would go deep into the desert, his eyes locked upon the heavens if he waited long enough he could see the passing of stars, comets, and constellations. In them were his dreams.

The feringi had two weeks, not one minute longer, more to give him that which he had demanded. Then the boy would watch his wife die slowly, a slice of her being taken away every day. Once there was nothing left of her but madness, he would start on the son of the arms dealer. Unless, of course, the old man reconsidered once he knew what had happened to the girl.

Taking a path up the side of the mountain, he passed sentries whose eyes sparkled with the fire of devotion above the folds of their veils.

"El kher ghas."

He acknowledged that all was well.

Sunni Ali found what he desired, a place where he could look out into the distance to where the hand of God touched the sky and the earth as one. It was good to let the great quiet seep into his soul. It was pure, clean. That is all that he wished for. He knew of the cities to the West and the Orient, of their sickness of soul and heart. He was no fool.

Let the outside world think of him as only another madman of the desert. He knew what he was doing. If the desert was to be returned to its rightful owners, now was the time.

The nations around them were weak. Recent wars of independence had taken all of the energies and resources of the colonial powers. They could not afford a war in the desert. Europe had its own problems and war and was weary. They had no interest in the Sahara, only in its oil. Even that could be negotiated. France was emotionally crippled by her long wars in Asia and North Africa. England had her own problems in Kenya and Egypt.

On his side also were many liberal organizations with over-worked social consciences to whom the return of the lands to their original peoples would seem a fine and good thing. All this he had as allies, and most of all he had the desert.

To wage war at this time, Sunni Ali could rally an army that would cost hundreds of millions to match, money which would not be easily forthcoming. From the Tuareg alone he could call on 70,000 warriors. If the Bedouin and rest of the Berber joined with him, they would number over 150,000 fighting men. A major force, a force larger than the combined armies of Algeria, Libya, and Tunisia.

He would leave the feringi their coastlines and green valleys, and make the cost of one hectare of his desert so high no man in his right mind would wish to pay the price for it. But it had to be now before the climate of the outside world changed and too many of the desert peoples were drawn into the cities and ruined by the corruption which was bred there.

It was a great dream, one he had first had when he became a convert to the ways of Allah, may His name be praised. Islam was the light, the flame which he would use to unite the tribes. His people, the Tuareg, were already devout Moslems. Among those who had come to him, he had slowly enforced the Islamic law of old by increasing the discipline a little every day. The pure faith of Mohammed would be vital to his plans, to give his men the singleness of thought and purpose which could unite them against the outsiders.

A wind blew from the southwest. He knew where it originated. On the ocean currents off the Ivory Coast. In his mind it still had the smell of the sea to it. Beyond this range the winds would be sucked dry as he would suck dry the bodies of any who came against him.

Removing his veil Sunni Ali bared his face to the crystal clear night, exposing his true self. If it had not been for the blue cast given it by the indigo dye, his face would have been as fair as the day his mother had given birth to him faraway in the green valley of the Rhine River.

The years had been long since the day he had escaped from the American prisoner of war camp outside of Tunis. He made his way into the desert and wandered about half-mad until he was found by a band of Tuaregs heading south across the Sahara away from the war. He had gone with them. He had been brought into the clan by their master, Bukush, a member of the Imahren, the upper caste of the Tuareg, through marriage to one of his daughters.

They taught him their ways and he aided them with his modern mind. He could make machinery work. He knew modern weapons and tactics. He should know, having once been a colonel in Rommel's Afrika Korps. He knew how to fight in the desert against the West.

Once Bukush died, Sunni Ali had slowly taken over guidance of the Azbine clan into which he had married and been adopted. By his command the Azbini had gone to the north and brought back items which had been abandoned on a dozen battlefields. He had repaired the vehicles, two Hanamog half-tracks and three American jeeps. These had been kept stored in the caves where he now held his captives.

For eleven long years they had waited. Their small stockpile of weapons and ammunition was not enough for his mission, but it was enough to secure his leadership. And Sunni Ali had a great advantage: a modern, trained mind to command warriors who still had the raw courage of the savage in their breasts. He would guide them, be their father, and make them a great people once more.

Yes, it was a good dream, one that he would follow to the end. For such was the will of God. *In sha' Allah!*

CHAPTER SIX

Monpelier and Dominic were waiting for Langers when he and Gus returned from Wadi Jebel. At two other tables were what Carl presumed to be the rest of the team.

He was glad he made it back at the time when the electricity was on and the ceiling fans were turning. Leaving the bar, Dominic and Monpelier joined him and Gus at a table directly under one of the rotating fans. To Dominic and Gus, Carl said, "Just to be on the safe side, spread out where you can keep an eye on things."

Dominic went to where he could see the lobby. Gus went to the bar, stationing himself behind the new arrivals. Carl faced off with Monpelier. Drinks were ordered, then Carl filled him in on what he had found out from Sharif Mamud.

Monpelier frowned. "I have heard the same. It bears out what I have learned. In essence, I have nothing else to add at this point. I wish we had time to plan this more carefully but we're running out of time. Planning ahead, I have already sent vehicles to Fort Laperrine. If you have no objections to the rest of the team, we'll pull out tomorrow by plane. We should arrive at about the same time, maybe a day earlier than those driving.''

''Looks like you have the logistics pretty well in hand. You must be getting a hell of a bonus if we pull this off.''

Monpelier shrugged. ''You know me, *mon vieux*. I am a humanitarian, interested only in returning those youngsters to the arms of their families.''

Carl couldn't have cared less. As long as his end of the bargain was lived up to, whatever side deal Monpelier had was his business.

''All right. What kind of aircraft do we have and what about weapons?'' Carl asked.

Monpelier leaned over the table. ''I have a Dakota C-47 in excellent flying condition. As for weapons: grenades, Browning 9 mm pistols for everyone, four Mats-49 submachine guns. The rest of the arms are American. They consist of one Browning automatic rifle and one 30 cal LMG. The rest of the team will be outfitted with Garand rifles. That way all the ammunition will be interchangeable except for the SMGs and pistols. I also have a 60 mortar with fifty rounds, and a bazooka. All the weapons are on the plane, which will be touching down here at dawn tomorrow.''

One thing Carl had always liked about working with Monpelier was that the man planned ahead and did it right. He had no doubt that all the equipment would be in excellent condition and ready for use.

"Good enough. Now fill me in on the team. Then I want to meet the men you have here. I presume the others are taking the vehicles south?"

"Yes, you are correct. Very well," Monpelier began. "The small, nervous-looking one with the thinning hair and mustache is Gerome Sims. He's English. He will be your medic; he is also proficient with most small arms. His prior service, former British eighth Army, then a bit of time with the Rhodesians and South Africans. He has some desert experience, naturally."

Carl knew what he meant. The eighth Army had been Field Marshall Montgomery's men in the North African Campaign. "The others?" he asked.

Monpelier sipped his drink. "They are of our sort, former legionnaires with no place to go. One is German, the other is, I believe, Spanish or possibly South American. I don't know for certain, but he calls himself a Spaniard, so that's that. His name is Roman Portrillo. He is a weapons man, a specialist with automatics. I would suggest giving him the BAR or the LMG.

"As for the German, Egon Stzchel. Ex-Wehrmacht. I believe he might have been an officer at one time; he has the look. At any rate, he is good with just about everything. A bit pushy but a good man when the shit gets deep. Like you and your animal, he is an alumnus of Russia. He has little real desert experience though, only what he got during training at Sidi Slimane. He was discharged for wounds in Indochina. Since then, I believe he has spent most of his time in the Orient.''

Monpelier ordered one more bottle of wine. ''The others with the transport are much the same; you will meet them at Fort Laperrine.''

Carl poured a glass of wine from the bottle. ''There will be one other going with us. Sharif Mamud. I want him and he wants to go. He knows the mountain and a way over it from the Tenere side.''

Monpelier glanced at the men at the table. ''Why does he want to go? Isn't he a bit long in the tooth for such a job?''

Carl nodded. ''Let's just say he has his reasons and I understand them. As for being long in the tooth, he can still out-march most men half his age and, like I said, he knows the area. That can be very important. It might make the difference in getting in and out alive.''

''*C'est bien*. If that's the way you want it, then I have no objections.''

''Good. I'll send Gus and Dominic over to get him in the morning. They should be back by dark.''

Monpelier drained the last of his glass. ''That will work out. When Mamud gets here we'll head out to the strip and load up. If we pull out at, say, four in the morning, we should be at the strip in Fort Laperrine around noon. It is twelve hundred kilometers, give or take a few."

Carl put his glass down. "What about landing at Laperrine. Are we going to have any problems?"

Monpelier rose, yawning. "Excuse me, my friend. My eyes feel like sand pits. But as to your question, there will be no trouble; we will have plenty of cooperation. That is one thing great wealth can usually buy. We will go in and refuel under the guise of being a geological survey crew looking for oil. And if anyone in authority thinks any different, they have but to radio their headquarters to be put in a cooperative mood. All has been prepared."

Carl agreed. "It seems like you've pretty well covered all bases. Go ahead and get some sleep. I'll introduce myself to the others."

"Very well. But please try not to piss them off until we are operational. It is too late to look for replacements. Therefore be tolerant and don't let Gus play games with them."

Carl laughed. "All right, Sergent Chef. We'll be good. Now go on and get out of my way. I have to meet them sooner or later."

Monpelier left the lounge feeling a bit uneasy as he saw Gus take down a liter of wine in one draught. But he had made Langers the boss. He would have to go along with him. This was no

time to start a split in the leadership and, of
course, he was not going all the way with them.
His job was, for the most part, complete once he
had them in their transport and on their way into
the desert. After that, the next time he saw them
would be when they were picked up and brought
back, hopefully successful. But if they were not?
He shrugged mentally. That was life, or death,
whichever the case turned out to be.

The three recruits sat quietly, knowing they had
been discussed. Now they waited to meet their
leader and size him up. The two former legionnaires had heard of Gus and Langers, and Roman
had even met Dominic at Sidi Bel Abbes.

Egon Stachel was a serious-looking man, hair
sun-bleached, eyes very pale blue. His mouth had
once been sensitive; now it was only a slash
through which he took sustenance and spoke. He
had grown dry with war. Roman was tall, handsome with a proud nose and dark eyes. He stood
over six feet and moved gracefully like one of the
famed dancers of Seville. Langers liked him on
the spot. Sims, the medic, sat patiently drinking
straight gin. A filthy habit, Carl thought, but then
no one had ever figured the English out. Sims
didn't seem to be at all interested in what was
going down.

"Gentlemen, I am Carl Langers. Monpelier
has told you about me. I am to be in command of
the actual operation. I only want one thing from
you and that's to do the job and do it right. Sup-

posedly you've all been around the horn, so I don't have to explain basics. Do as I say when I say it, that's all. Once we're committed, there will not be time for arguments. If you have anything to contribute, do it before we move out into the desert. I'll listen, but I make the final decisions and they are not debatable.

"I have known Monpelier for years. He is one of the best organizers in the business. If he says he has something then he does. All the equipment is ready and will be on site when we need it. There will be one other going with us, an Arab sheik who knows the terrain. I trust him, therefore you will trust him."

He ran his eyes over them as he spoke, looking for any signs of nervousness or fear. There were none. Roman's face was a bit flushed but Carl put that down to excitement, not fear. The German looked intense but not upset. Carl knew that he and Egon would have to have a talk in private later. Sims just smiled in acceptance of whatever conditions were to be imposed. He didn't like responsibility anyway, and whoever was in command was fine with him, as long as he knew his job. And it certainly appeared that this scar-faced man did. Therefore he was satisfied.

Egon spoke first. "What is to be the chain of command?"

Carl eyed him. "We'll settle that when I meet the rest of the team."

Gus and Dominic came over to stand casually

behind Langers. They said nothing, but their presence reinforced his authority in Egon's mind. "As you say, sir," Egon toasted him with an empty glass. "What are our orders for now?"

To all of them Carl said, "Just be ready to move out when I say so. It could be anytime, so don't bother unpacking your gear. Stay off the booze and leave the locals alone. You are all restricted to the hotel unless I tell you otherwise. No phone calls and no trouble. As of now we have had our last drink until the job is over."

Egon stood. His frame was slender but well muscled. He bowed his head slightly, accepting the commands. Roman put the cork back into the bottle of wine he'd been sipping and Sims sighed with deep regret as he neatly tossed off the last of the gin.

"That's it for now. Once we have the rest of the team together we'll go over the actual mission and the time schedule. Till we pull out, stay together when you're out of your rooms and if any tourists show up, we're going out on a survey job for an oil company. If they get any nosier, tell them the company doesn't like you talking about your work. They'll understand that. If they persist refer them to me.

"That's it. I'll see you all tomorrow. I am sure you are all tired after the day's trip. Rest well."

They accepted their dismissal with good grace. Egon looked back as they left the bar and saw Gus starting to pour another drink.

''That goes for you too, Gus,'' Carl snapped. ''No more booze till we're through.'' Gus grunted something obscene and carefully poured the drink back into its bottle and screwed the cap on.

Egon smiled. He liked what he saw. Langers would enforce the same rules on everyone. That was good. It saved problems in the future. Yes, Langers would probably do quite well. He wondered if they'd served on the same front in Russia.

CHAPTER SEVEN

Sharif Mamud was picked up by Gus and Dominic early in the morning. True to his word, the old man was ready to go, waiting in front of his tent with his single sack of personal effects. They promptly headed back to Ghudamis. It was nearly three in the afternoon when they returned to the Saharienne.

Monpelier had requisitioned the town's only taxi to take Egon, Roman, and Sims over to the airstrip. The other four followed in the Land Rover. Monpelier's Dakota was inside one of the strip's two hangars. The pilot and copilot, Browning 9 mm automatics on their hips, were guarding the cargo inside the plane, which was worth a fortune. They stayed with the aircraft while Monpelier paid the taxi and assembled his team.

"I know it's a bit early in the game but I would rather have you all here," he explained. "That way, if anything goes down wrong we'll all be together and not spread out. Inside the plane is the equipment: weapons, uniforms, medical supplies, as well as radios, rations, and water.

From this time on, guard this plane with your life. That's all from me. Your pilots, Captain Parrish and Cocaptain Rigsby, have been briefed. They know what they are to do. In the air your captain is the boss. Other than that you will, of course, do as I said earlier and take your orders from Mr. Langers.''

Parrish looked over his passengers with a jaded eye. They were a rough-looking crew, especially the gorilla beside the one called Langers. Parrish was not unimpressive himself. With wavy, premature pure silver hair, he stood six feet six at 227 pounds. He could carry his own weight in most circumstances, but Gus bothered him. The beast fit no category he had ever seen before. When he watched the big German move he had a sudden urge to offer him a banana, but he wisely resisted the temptation when Gus casually picked up a fifty-five gallon oil drum and moved it over to where he could sit on it in the shade. The drum was full.

Carl called Monpelier over to him. "I want to take a look at the gear. Do you have an inventory list with you?''

"Go right ahead. There is a list in the box marked medical. I'll just wait out here with the others. It's too hot inside the plane.''

Before climbing inside the Dakota, Carl told Dominic, "Take Stachel with you and keep an eye posted outside. Let me know if anything looks suspicious or if we're going to have any company.''

Boxes lined the center of the plane, tied down with retaining straps. Looking them over he found the one marked medical. Releasing it from its strap, he opened the box up. On top was the list. He read it over. Monpelier had done good. Cracking the lids on the boxes containing the weapons, he examined every piece. All were brand new. A voice behind him coughed politely.

''I say, would you mind terribly if I had a quick look at my kit? I want to make certain that nothing we might need later has been left out.''

Carl nodded at Sims and pointed out the medic box. Sims fluttered over it, humming as he unpacked it, carefully laying everything out in order: antibiotics, battle dressings, salt tablets, a minor surgery kit, and even several IV setups. When he was done he carefully placed everything back in proper order.

''Well now, it seems as if it's all here. I do hope that I don't have to put any of it to use but then, it is better to be prepared, what?''

Carl sat down on a box of ammo and said, ''Tell me a bit about yourself, Mr. Sims.''

The medic cocked an eye and sat down by the open cargo door. ''Not much to say really. I've kicked about a bit. Africa with Monty, then a turn or two in the south, Rhodesia and the Congo. You know that wherever you types go, there always has to be someone like me to try and patch you up a bit. I did have two years of medical school, but circumstances dictated that I depart from those hallowed halls. Though I would one day like to go back.'' He sighed deeply. ''Ah, but life takes its own hand in the game and who knows? I am content enough. That's about it, sir.''

Carl lit up a smoke, offered one to Sims but was politely refused.

''You ever work with any of the others here?'' Carl asked.

Sims nodded his head. ''Only with Egon. Herr Stachel is not a bad sort. He looks like a bloody Prussian, but he's all right. Does his job and is selective about who he works for. Won't just take anything for money. We were in the south together for a few months. He's steady and will be where you need him. I don't really think he cares much about whether he lives or dies. Some men, you know, are always ready for the last game, even anticipating it. He is one of those, but he won't do anything that jeopardizes the rest of the team.''

Carl was glad to hear that. The last thing he needed was a hard-headed former Nazi with something to prove.

''The Spaniard?''

Sims shook his head in the negative. ''Don't know a thing about him, love. But he seems a good sort. I only hope he's not one of those hot-blooded Latins who always settles minor quarrels with knives.'' He shuddered at the thought.

Carl got up. ''Good enough. We'll all get a chance to know each other a bit better before this job is over.''

Back in the hangar Gus and Stachel were speaking in German, finding that they had only one thing in common and that was the Russian front. Calling Gus over to him Carl said, ''Take it easy on these boys, Gus. I don't want any broken bones. Like Monpelier said, it's too late to get any replacements.''

Gus laughed. ''Uncle Gus wouldn't harm the hair on a fly's head. You know that. Besides which, I like Herr Stachel, even if he was once a member of the officer class. May all their children have terminal hemorrhoids.''

Carl just shook his head. There simply wasn't much that could be done with Gus. Going over to Sharif Mamud, he took his bag and removed the photos that Monpelier had given him from it.

''Want to take a look at these?''

Sharif Mamud took the pictures and examined them closely. When he came to the one Monpelier had said he thought was the area where Sunni Ali had the captives held, Carl pointed it out to Mamud. ''Know this place?''

Squinting his eyes, Mamud moved closer to the hangar door for a better look. ''Yes. I have been there. It is a good place with water inside the caves and many tunnels to hide in. It is very old. Inside are pictures of many animals who have long since left the desert. They were drawn when the Sahara was covered with grass. Very, very old indeed.''

Carl took the photo from him. It was one taken before the war. That didn't bother him. It wasn't likely that things had changed. He took his map out and he handed it over to Mamud. ''Show me exactly where this cave is located.''

Mamud spread the map on the floor of the hangar. Taking a moment to orient himself, he touched the map with a forefinger. ''There, near the southern end. It is a place well suited for defense. If I were you I would consider the possibility of coming in from some place on the other side, as I told you earlier. It will take longer but you will have a better chance. Sunni Ali and the Tuaregs think there is no one but them who can survive in the desert or cross the mountains. It is a vanity of theirs which has, in the past, proved fatal more than once.''

Carl nodded. ''Let's hope this is one more time.''

Parrish was talking to Monpelier, who nodded agreement and announced, ''All right, gentlemen, let's get aboard. It's time to move out. Our captain said that the weather report indicates there is a strong head wind approaching which may slow us up a bit. If he's right, then we'll have to leave now in order to make it to the strip outside of Fort Laperrine by dawn.''

As they climbed on board, Parrish told them to

secure their personal effects in the rear of the plane and then sit down. There were only canvas seats of the military type, not very comfortable for a long haul. But after they were airborne, they'd be able to move about or even lie down in the aisle to sleep if they chose to.

The copilot opened the hangar doors all the way and climbed back in to take his place in the copilot's seat. The twin engine started smoothly with no hesitation. That always made one feel a bit better about flying. Parrish taxied out to the runway, checked the wind sock, faced into it, and took off without further ceremony. There was no tower control. You just came in and left when you thought you could make it. Carl took a seat in front of the wing on the port side. The plane gained altitude easily heading its nose south, deep into the heartland of the sea of dunes.

The flight was long and monotonous. Parrish turned on the heaters. At 11,000 feet it was near the freezing point when the sun fell. The night was clear; the winds were yet in front of them. Below Carl could see the dunes, dark waves of sand that moved with the winds. Some were hundreds of feet high. There was nothing but the mountains to resist the movement of the sands and even those would in time be worn away by the hard, polished grains that came every day, century after century, to chip away at the stones.

Parrish knew the area well, at least from the sky, anyway. He'd been flying the African circuit for the last ten years, from Pretoria to Benghazi. Checking the time, he knew exactly where they were, the southern edge of the Great Eastern Erg. The sand waves were less dominant here and he couldn't see them anymore. The earth below was scarred by pale brown ridges and gorges, sandstone and granite ranges that expanded and contracted under the alternating heat and cold of the Sahara. If front of them was the Tassili N'Ajers, a low range of mountains where thousands of wall paintings had been found. Another hour and half from there and they would come to the Ahaggar range with Mount Tahat rising up over 9,000 feet.

He would swing around the range. If his timing was right, they would hit the head winds before then. He didn't want to get caught in the upper air currents, which raged at times over the high peaks. Parrish would play it safe. He'd swing a bit to the left and come from the south into Fort Lapperine, or as the nomads called the city by the fort, Tamanrasset. From the south two roads led into the city, one from Niger and the other from Mali. He had used them as guides more than once and was glad that he never had to make the trip by land.

The inside of the plane was lit by a red light. Parrish looked back at the men sitting or lying asleep on the deck and wondered how many of them he would be taking back out. He had been on jobs like this before and knew that when he returned his plane would be lighter than when he had come. Some of them back there were probably dead men.

"Rigsby, take her for a while. I'm going to get some shut-eye. Wake me when we get near the Ahaggar Mountains."

Rigsby grunted an affirmative reply, which was about all he ever did. He was a short, dark, barrel-chested, taciturn man of Irish descent who had little use for any conversation that wasn't absolutely necessary.

After taking one last look at the gauges and instruments, Parrish shut his eyes and leaned his head back against the cushions of his seat. Rigsby didn't say much, but he was a hell of pilot. As good as he was. Well, almost.

Those in the rear had their own thoughts, all except Gus, who had as near to a complete vacuum as the human mind could produce. The rest half-slept as the Dakota sailed through the wine-colored skies of the African night. Nowhere on earth were the nights so clear and the stars so bright.

Carl leaned his head against the side of the plane, letting the vibrations seep into his flesh. It was steady, almost comforting in its trembling rhythm. He knew this land, too. In his mind he could hear the trampling of the Roman Legions as they formed the battle square, the war cries of Crusaders who fought for the glory of Jesus and plunder. And the nomads: Moors, Berbers,

Tuaregs, and Arabs who had swept out of the deserts crying out for all to hear: *"La ilah illa' Allah: Muhammad rasul Allah.* There is no god but Allah: Mohammed is His prophet."

The only way the sand below could have ever bloomed would have been if blood were as nourishing as water. Rivers of blood had flowed from those who had tried to claim the desert, floods that had claimed millions of lives instead. So what difference would a few more drops spilled onto the sands in the next few days make? Carl answered the question before sleep hit him: None. *Malesh.*

CHAPTER EIGHT

The Dakota C-47 lurched a bit when Parrish
banked it to the port. The head winds had reached
them, slowing the plane's ground speed down to a
little over a hundred miles per hour. For the next
hour the plane bucked and rocked, swayed and
dipped. Those lying on the floor woke up and sat
back in their seats where they had the comfort of
safety belts.

Parrish would have liked to go higher but his
plane wasn't pressurized. Still he took it up to
12,000 feet. That was it. He had oxygen for himself and Rigsby but if he went any higher some of
the guys in the back would start to pass out.

Gaining 1,000 feet helped a bit. At least he'd
gotten above the sandstorm. Below him it was as
though the floor of the desert had come up to meet
him. It was a solid sheet of darkness sweeping
past him. If he had stayed down lower it would
have sandblasted his plane down to the frame.

He told Rigsby to tune in Radio Niamey for the
weather report.

"Looks like the storm should be over in another hour or two, boss."

Parrish was glad. The plane was kept in good repair, but one never knew. The remote possibility of having to go down in winds of over fifty miles per hour with zero visibility was less than appealing.

"Glad to hear that. We'll just ride it out till it passes, then go in. By then we should have first light. I don't want to go down till then, anyway."

Rigsby jerked his head to the rear. "What do you think about those guys back there?"

Parrish shrugged his shoulders. "Who knows. I'm just glad we're not going with them. It's bad enough hauling this crate around for a living."

Rigsby grunted in agreement. "Yeah, but it still seems a bit strange. You know, taking these guys in and knowing that not all of them will be coming back. Strange, kinda like we're a hearse rented in advance."

Parrish leaned back to get more comfortable. "Knock it off, Rigsby. They got their job to do and we got ours. Don't think too much about them. They're expendable. That's why they're here, and they know it. But I would like to think that we're not, so just keep this bucket's nose in the wind and off the deck till then. I'm going to try and catch a few winks."

"You got it, boss. I'll wake you at first light. That should be in about two more hours." Rigsby took over the yoke.

Carl watched the faces of his men as they tried to sleep through the buffeting of the air currents. Gus was the only one who slept peacefully, his head bobbing and jerking from side to side as the plane rode the bumps. Sharif Mamud looked a bit green, maybe had a touch of airsickness. Carl checked his watch. Dawn would be coming soon. His eyes closed.

The winds below began to slacken until they didn't have enough force to keep the grains of sand flying. The storm was dying with the new day. The earth was still dark but to the west Rigsby saw the sun edging up over the rim of the world.

"Wake up, boss." He nudged Parrish. "Time to put this crate down."

Parrish stretched in his seat, trying to work out the kinks in his back. He extended his long arms, nearly hitting his copilot in the face. "Sorry about that. Okay, I got her. Now let's take her in." They were 100 miles off course, which was no big deal. The Ahaggar Mountains could easily be seen off to the starboard.

Parrish banked to the port and lined up on the southern end of the range. "One hour till touchdown. Hope they got some coffee at the strip."

Carl's eyes came open when he heard the landing gear being lowered. The plane shuddered a bit, then steadied.

The sky was crystal clear, visibility unlimited. Parrish made one pass over the runway to check the wind sock. It was calm, though sudden gusts could blow up at any time. The strip had been cut by bulldozers leveling off a small mountaintop during the time when Fort Laperrine had been one of colonial France's southernmost outposts. Nothing had changed since the last time Parrish had been there: a few huts with metal roofs, a couple of frame hangars, some fuel tanks, and a building that had once housed a poor-man's control center. Now it was abandoned.

Lining the nose up he lowered his flaps to full and cut back on the throttle. One good thing about the C-47 was that it had a hell of a good glide factor with the cool morning air. He set it down easy, smoothly cut the power, and taxied straight to one of the hangars. Off to the side of the runway were a few goats under the care of shepherd boys, their eyes large with wonder as the plane coasted in.

As they taxied Rigsby hit the intercom mike, announcing to his passengers in the rear: "Ladies and gentlemen, welcome to lovely Fort Laperrine, onetime romantic outpost of the Foreign Legion, now host to an unknown number of ghosts and goatherds. While our captain taxies us in, please remain in your seats and observe the no smoking sign until we have come to a complete stop, at which time stay where you are, pending further instructions. Thank you for flying with us, and we hope we have made your trip as much a pleasure for you as it has been for us to serve you.'' Parrish looked at Rigsby with raised eye-brows. He hadn't said that much at one time since Parrish had known him. Rigsby just shrugged.

Rigsby's impression of an airline stewardess did much to set a good mood. It lightened the moment. As they taxied down the runway Carl looked out the porthole. There were three other aircraft visible, another Dakota and a couple of single-engine Cessnas. None of them had military or government markings.

Monpelier went to the cargo door and pulled it open, then leaned out to get a look around. Carl wondered who he was expecting. He didn't think the other crew in the Land Rovers could have made it in that fast, not with the storm of last night.

When they came to a stop in front of the open doors of a frame hangar with a tin roof and peeling gray paint, he heard a hail from the ground.

"Marhava yessun. Welcome, effendis, to Tamanraset.''

Monpelier greeted the turbaned man in a threadbare white suit, with:

"Allah maak, Yousef.''

"And God be with you also, Mr. Monpelier. All is as you requested. Please to leave your transport and feel at ease.''

Monpelier pulled his head back inside "It's okay, he works for me.'' Carl saw him adjust a bulge under his shirt the size of one of the 9 mm before jumping down to the ground. Gus looked at

Carl who gave him the nod. Gus took one of the Mats-49 SMGs out of its box and slapped a loaded magazine in it. When he did this, the rest of the crew instantly cleared any fog from their brains and were on the edge of their seats, ready to move.

"Sit still. I'm just playing it safe," Carl said. Gus moved to where he could keep an eye on Monpelier and Yousef, who was escorting Monpelier into the hangar.

Gus kept the submachine gun out of sight but ready to fire if needed. Monpelier went over to a few crates and drums, inspecting them, nodding his head up and down, then waved for the rest of them to come on in.

Carl stretched his legs before leaving. To the rest of the men he ordered, "Break out the pistols. Fill clips and take them with you but keep them out of sight. When you leave the aircraft, move loose and easy but place yourselves where we can keep an eye out for a full 360 degrees. Like I said earlier, I'm just playing it safe. Gus, you stay with the plane until I send someone to relieve you. I wouldn't want any of our cargo to disappear or get into the wrong hands."

The men did as he ordered and casually spread out. Carl followed Monpelier inside the hangar and found him talking to the Arab who had greeted him, a tall, thin man with hot eyes and long delicate fingers, wearing his white tropical business suit which had long since seen better days.

"This is Yousef, an old acquaintance of mine, Carl. He is a very useful man as long as you can outbid your competition. But at least he doesn't make any bones about it. You always know where you stand with him."

Carl nodded to the Arab. "Then he won't have any hard feelings if I let him know that if he does anything that screws up our job I will find him and kill him in a way that his ancestors would have appreciated."

Monpelier grinned widely. He always liked to provoke a reaction where he could. It made the job so much more interesting. Yousef had a wary look to him as he tried and failed to meet the gaze of the scar-faced man.

"He means it, Yousef. He will find you and do exactly as he has said he would. Perhaps you heard of him during the troubles. Some of your people gave him a nickname, al-Kattel, the killer. Does that ring a bell, old boy?"

Monpelier was obviously delighted with Yousef's reaction. Suddenly sweat beads appeared on his brow and upper lip. A slight nervous tremor shook the hand that wiped the sweat away with a yellowish handkerchief. He had heard of al-Kattel.

"*La, ya akhi!* You misjudge me, sirs. I am an honorable man doing only my very best for my friends. I assure you that I am here only to serve your needs. See, have I not delivered to this most difficult and lonely place all that you asked of me?'' He indicated the fuel drums and supplies. ''In the office I have also installed, as per your instructions, the radio. It is a most fine radio, sir. With it you can speak to the whole world if you should so desire. Please do not think that I would break our long friendship by a hasty act.''

Monpelier had to control a burst of laughter that had started low in his gut and threatened to explode out his mouth. He swallowed to keep it down and said quite seriously, ''I know that, old friend. And now I am certain that your new acquaintance will become a good friend to you also, providing you both live long enough to learn to appreciate each other's good points.''

Nodding his head at what had once been the hangar office he said, ''Come with me. We might as well get as comfortable as possible.''

As they headed for the office, Parrish and Rigsby were already checking over their plane, getting it ready for the next flight. They wouldn't lie down until that was done. They'd learned from past experience that it was best to be ready for an instant takeoff.

The office still held some furniture, a rolltop desk, two cane chairs, and a couch whose leather cushions had cracked and dried. Carl chose a chair.

Monpelier went to the desk, on which sat the radio. He turned it on to check it out. Satisfied, he turned it back off. ''This is so I can keep in contact with you for most of the time and perhaps be able to provide any extra assistance you might need.

There will be one more like this with the Land Rovers.''

They were interrupted by Sims sticking his head in the door. ''I say, sir. Your man, you know, the big brute, is asking about food and drink. What should I tell him?''

Carl looked at Monpelier, who said, ''Tell him to come on in. Yousef has provided for that as well. Find him and tell him to get everyone fed.''

Sims looked at Carl for confirmation. After all, he was their leader now.

Carl nodded in agreement. ''Go ahead, Sims, and tell the others to take it easy but keep an eye out. Also, I want the crates with the weapons brought inside. The rest of the gear can stay on the plane.''

''Very good, sir.''

Sims disappeared to do as he was told.

Monpelier grunted. ''Very conscientious, that one, *n'est-ce pas?*''

''Yes, I think he'll do all right. But right now I would like to know when the rest of the team will be in. That storm will probably have slowed them down.''

Monpelier agreed. ''You are right, of course, but if they haven't had any motor trouble, even with the storm they should be in by nightfall or early morning at the latest. If you want to rest some more there'll be some sleeping bags among the gear that Yousef brought. They're good ones—American army.''

''Not right now. I'll wait a while.''

Carl left Monpelier in the office. He wanted to get outside for a while. Here in the Ahaggars the air was cooler. At night it would drop to freezing quite often. Just out of sight behind a ridge was Fort Laperrine. He had been there before, years ago when they had fought the Tuaregs and Riff raiders that had been driven from the Atlas Mountains into the desert. The town was like all the others. For centuries it had been a juncture where caravans could rest and water. Whoever controlled the Ahaggars controlled access to the heart of the Algerian Sahara. *"Vive la Légion."*

He nearly laughed. When he thought about it he had enough time in the Legion to collect a half-dozen pensions. A shiver rippled over his forearms. The Ahaggars had never meant anything but trouble, and now he was back. He wanted to get out of them as soon as possible.

Nothing to do but wait for the others to show up. If they didn't make it in time then what? Would he be able to go in with what he had? Not likely but not impossible, if they had a death wish. It was hard as hell to scare men who were ready to die. He knew he had at least one, Dominic . . . and maybe Sharif Mamud.

CHAPTER NINE

They spent the night in the hangar, Carl and Dominic questioning Sharif Mamud about the mountain. It was an hour after dawn when the Land Rovers showed up. The passengers were heavily coated with Saharan dust. They looked more like ghosts than mercenaries.

Monpelier had them pull the Land Rovers inside the hangar. Carl didn't envy them their journey. It had to have been a ball-buster. From the way they moved he knew they had the same opinion.

The stiff-legged arrivals accepted Monpelier's invitation and headed for some water cans to rinse off before getting down to business. Among them was Abdul Khanas. He was one Carl had met before, a Sudanese veteran of Indochina, a good, solid man with strong hands and a quick smile. The only other one he knew was Jacques Foche, a Belgian mercenary who had been with nearly all the world's armies at one time or another. He was without conscience or loyalty to anyone or anything except the job he was on at the time.

The rest of the team consisted of two Brits, Felix Martine and Kitchner, an American named Alan Graves, and Saul Voorhees from Pretoria.

It was obvious that some of them had worked together before. Abdul greeted Roman warmly and gave Egon a nod of recognition. Dominic made the rest of the introductions.

Carl told them to rack out for a while. After that ride they were sure to need it and he didn't want anyone falling asleep when he outlined the job.

At four in the afternoon the men had been fed and their coffee poured. They found seats on boxes and crates, and were waiting.

"Some of you know me," Carl began. "We have worked together before. Those of you who have questions about me, go with them to those that have worked with me. I don't have time for individual consultations.

"Monpelier has told you the purpose of the job: to get in, snatch two people, and get back out. Let's try to do it and return with everyone that we started out with. Tomorrow the Land Rovers will move out again with new crews." There was an audible sigh of relief from those who had just driven over 1,000 miles across the desert. "They'll have radios with them so we'll know when they're on site. They are to find a landing zone for the rest of us to set down on. Those in the Land Rovers will have only one rifle and their pistols for personal protection. If they carried any more with them they'd be too tempting a target for bandits. When they are on site they'll signal and we'll move out. Till then everyone is restricted to the strip and this hangar. No one goes into town. If one word leaks out about the job then the whole thing will be blown and someone's definitely going to die.'' He waited to give them time to digest what he was saying.

''All right, then. A lot of this is going to have to be played by ear. We know where the hostages are being held and we have a guide who knows the terrain and will lead us in. Once on site, anything can happen. At last word there were about forty to fifty armed Tuaregs at the target area. I don't think that should slow us up any. They're tough, brave men, but I think we have experience and training on our side plus the advantage of surprise if we move fast enough. Just remember when we do go in follow orders and we'll have a good chance of pulling it off. There are still some details to be worked out and I'll fill you in on them when the time comes. As of right now, no one backs out. Everyone here is going all the way. Any questions?''

Egon stood up. ''What is our time frame?''

Carl looked at Dominic, who held up his hand. ''We have five days max. Then Sunni Ali is going to start sending little pieces of the girl to her father-in-law. We want to get to them before that happens.''

''All right,'' Carl said, ''let me run it down. As

it stands now we go in from the desert side of the mountain. We hit them before dawn. Grab the boy and girl, and run for it. The Land Rovers will be waiting to rendezvous and pick us up. We'll ride to where the plane can set down, load up, and get out. That's it. Simple and easy if nothing goes down wrong, which will depend a great deal on you people. That's it for now. No more questions till later.

"I want Dominic, Stachel, Roman, and Sims to come with me to the office."

The group broke up. The men he called off followed him into the hangar office and sat on the couch and chairs.

"Okay, you guys are it," Carl told them. "You're going for a little ride. Dominic, you're in charge." He spread out a map of the area and showed Dominic where he wanted him to be. "I need two landing zones, one somewhere around here," he pointed to the western side of Mt. Baguezane, "and the other landing zone here near the road leading from Agadez to the Ahaggars."

He folded up the map and gave it to Dominic. "I want you to go out and check out the Land Rovers. Talk to the new guys and see if they had any problems with them. Give them the full treatment. Oil change and filters, and don't take any chances with them on the road. We can't afford any breakdowns. If you're wondering why I'm sending you, I think that's obvious. You're rested; those guys out there are beat. I'm keeping

Gus with me because he'd attract too much attention out there. He's just too damned noticeable."

They all had to admit that was true. To Egon, Carl said, "Monpelier told me that you had radio training. Is that right?"

"Yes, I can handle most kinds of communication equipment," Egon replied.

"Good. I want a check-in every eight hours, beginning at 0800 hours around the clock. Sims, I'm sending you because I want these men in good shape when the rest of us get there. So take care of them. Roman, from what Dominic has told me you're the best shooter, but try to avoid any trouble. If it comes I don't want anyone getting out to tell. If you have to shoot, then kill.

"Right now I want you men to do like I said, check out the vehicles and draw supplies. Check everything out yourselves, then report back to me. That's it for now. Get on with it."

When Carl opened the door to let them out, he saw Yousef standing by the Land Rovers talking with the new arrivals. He had not been present at the meeting and that was at Carl's request. Yousef had no idea what the details of the job were and Carl preferred to keep it that way.

"Yousef! Come here," he ordered.

The frame in the white suit visibly shrank at the sound of his name. Scuttling over to Carl he tried to affect an open, friendly stance. "Ah yes, effendi, is there something I may do for you?"

"Yes, keep the hell away from those men. Don't talk to them, don't ask questions, and if you hear anything, forget it. Also, you will not be going anywhere for the next few days. You'll be staying right here with us."

"But, Effendi, I have much business to attend. Things which require my attention. I cannot remain here for such a time."

Langers grasped him by the wrist and applied pressure. Yousef felt the bones begin to give way. Through tears welling up in his eyes he croaked out, "But of course, sir. If you think it is best, then I shall certainly do as you request."

"Order, Yousef, not request." He released the wrist and left Yousef standing alone rubbing his injured limb with tender fingers, his eyes shooting daggers at Langers's back.

Monpelier had watched the scene and said while lighting a smoke, "You didn't make a friend with that routine."

"I really don't give a damn, Monpelier. There's something about him that I don't like."

Monpelier blew a smoke ring. "All I can say is that I've worked with him before and as long as he was well paid, I never had any trouble with him."

"Any trouble you knew about." Carl left him to chew that over.

For hours Dominic and the others toiled over the Land Rovers. It was near midnight before they turned in. Carl wanted them to have a good night's sleep before they headed out. The night's sentry duties were broken down among the new arrivals, with Gus taking first turn. Carl chose the last watch so he could see Dominic and the others off.

Monpelier had taken off with Parrish and the plane, saying he'd be back in a couple of days. He had business in Tripoli to attend to. That was all right. Carl needed a couple of days to get familiar with the new men, to watch them and locate trouble spots before they sprang up. One good thing was that this job was moving so fast there wouldn't be much time for personality conflicts to develop.

The new men had hit the rack early, trying to catch up on sleep, each taking a sleeping bag and making a place to lie down. Langers wandered around until a little after midnight, then lay down himself in the office. Rank did have its privileges; he took the couch.

Voorhees, the South African, woke Langers by tapping him lightly on the bottom of his foot. "Time to get up, sir." Langers grunted and rolled out shaking the kinks out of his back. Taking the submachine gun from Voorhees, he let him have the couch.

Dominic and the others were already up and ready. "All set, Carl. Is there anything else we need to know?"

Langers yawned widely before answering, "No. Just make sure you check in. Your call sign is Gold and I'm Silver. That ought to keep it simple enough. Remember we have to be on the deck in three days, no more. So don't fart around out there, and good luck."

Dominic took the lead, Sims drove the trailing vehicle, Egon was in the center with Roman. Their Land Rovers were loaded with extra gas and water cans as well as spare parts for those most likely to break down. Each vehicle had a power winch and cable on its front. These would be needed in the days to come when one would have to pull the other out of ruts and deep sand.

Langers watched them move out across the runway and out onto the road leading down the mountain to the flat lands. Three days, no more. If anything at all went wrong and slowed them up, there'd be hell to pay. He'd be glad when Monpelier got back. Gus was all right, but he wanted someone a bit more discreet on hand to keep an eye on Yousef. Gus had all the subtlety of an elephant in heat.

He was waiting by the radio when the first call came in right on time. The transmission was loud and clear.

"Silver, this is Gold. How do you read me? Over."

Langers hit the talk button. "I got you five by five. Everything okay?"

"Roger that, Silver. Making good time. The road is clear but it's getting hot as hell out here. Will check in again on schedule. Out."

Langers felt relief. It was good to get the first call, but he knew that from now until they rendezvoused he would wait impatiently for each check-in and worry like hell when they were a minute late.

During the next two days Yousef made it a point to keep out of his way. He found odd jobs to do and made no further requests of Langers for anything, knowing they would be refused. He was not going to be permitted to leave and that was that.

Langers talked with the rest of the team and, satisfied that each knew his job, left them pretty much to their own devices, cards, and talk of women. But no booze. From now until the job was over they would have a dry camp.

It quickly became a ritual for the men to hang around at check-in time. So far they'd had no problems to slow them down. The weather had been good and the vehicles performed perfectly. They had turned off the road on the Algerian side of the border to avoid the border checkpoint at Guezzam where Sunni Ali was certain to have eyes. They headed cross-country to pass into Niger, then turned back to the south to enter the Tenere depression. They were on time.

Carl was relieved when Monpelier returned with the plane. The only thing he'd been able to do in the last two days was have the men go over the gear, and you could only clean a weapon so many times. The reports from Dominic were the only real entertainment he had.

When Monpelier came back Carl collared him.

"It looks like a go. Dominic will find a place to set down and we'll go in tomorrow."

Monpelier wiped his face with the back of his sleeve. The day was warming up even here, 5,000 feet above sea level. "Very good. How have the men been behaving?"

"No problems, but I wouldn't want to keep them locked up here much longer. Did you find out anything else?"

"Yes, but I don't think it's going to please you. Understand that it is just a rumor, but Sunni Alli is supposed to have some kind of motor transport with him. Just what it is I don't know, and I also don't know where it's kept. So once you get the hostages out, don't waste any time. Move out fast."

"You can bank on it," Carl answered sourly. "I'll tell the men that we go in tomorrow morning after we hear from Dominic."

CHAPTER TEN

The salt flat shimmered. Heat waves rose in undulating crests, creating updrafts on which vultures rode with wide-spread wings. Dominic looked to the skies, checking the time. It should be any minute. To the south, dust devils whirled and rose, dancing across the furnace of heaven. Out on the flat there was even less life. Scorpions and snakes tended to avoid it. Few plants were hardy enough to survive. It was a place as dead as could be found anywhere on the planet.

At the north end the other two heavy-duty Land Rovers waited. Only Dominic stood at the southern end of the flat. He had driven over the landing site, making certain there was no unseen boulder that would burst a tire, no hidden ditch that could cause the plane to crash. He needn't have bothered. The flat was nearly as smooth as tarmac and almost as hard. The team of Land Rovers had spread out to provide security for the landing site. It wasn't likely anyone would be watching them but then again, who could tell. In clear, dry air, visibility was nearly unlimited. A man twenty miles away with sharp eyes could have focused on them.

The trip had been long, hot, and difficult over trails that even goats would avoid. Several times they'd had to stop to either pull one of the vehicles out of a sand trap or use the strips of perforated steel plating they had brought with them to dig down under the tires and pull themselves out.

Dominic would have liked to take his shirt off but that would have been foolish. His tender skin would have developed second-degree burns in a matter of minutes. The glare of the salt flats was eye piercing and the sun was only reflected and amplified by its whiteness.

His body tried to cool itself by sweating; it did no good. As soon as moisture appeared on his lips or face it was gone, evaporated. The sweat that reached his shirt lasted little longer. When it was gone it left white streaks from his own body salts soaked into the material.

Dominic put on dark glasses to ease the strain under the brim of his hat. He liked the desert; it felt good. The aching white was a comfort. For many the silence that could come to the barren lands was maddening. Not for him. It felt good. Clean.

He felt better now that he was going to work. That was what he needed, and the desert was a good place for killing. And for dying. It had been too long since he was operational. He knew that something had started to go wrong with him in

Indochina at Dien Bien Phu. A need to fight, not just kill, though that was an important part of it. Even his strong desire for women had diminished. Though he still enjoyed a little ass, it didn't have the same satisfaction to it unless he had been in battle. He knew that Carl and Gus were worried about him. But there was no need for such concern. He would not last much longer. Like Carl and Gus, he too had known men like himself who had become infected with the same disease he now carried in his soul. They had all died sooner than their compatriots. And it was almost always a violent death.

He laughed out loud. The sound startled him; it was so unnatural in this place of silence. Maybe he would die this time. The thought of his own termination didn't upset Dominic at all. It gave him only a vague feeling of curiosity as to what would come next, if anything. Either way it didn't matter. *He* didn't matter anymore. He was like the others with the death sickness. He was just waiting, waiting for a time and place to die . . . .

One more check of his watch. It was time to try and make contact. Getting on the radio he adjusted the squelch, set the frequency, and hit the talk button.

"Silver. This is Gold. Do you read me? Over."

Only static responded. He fine-tuned the frequency and turned up the volume.

"Silver, this is Gold. Do you read me? Over."

This time the response was a welcome voice,

crackling a bit, requiring him to adjust the squelch.

"Roger that, Gold. This is Silver. We are on our approach. How is it there?"

"Wind from the south about ten to fifteen. The deck is clear. Come on in, the party's waiting."

"Roger on that, Gold. Wind from the south ten to fifteen. Party is ready to play. Should be on the deck in ten. Do you roger that? Over."

"Roger, on deck in ten. Out."

Switching channels he spoke to the rest of the crew, reaching them on the walkie-talkies. "Okay out there, keep your eyes and ears open. Silver is coming in. Let's not get careless. Keep your eyes off the strip and on the desert. We could still get company. Some of you never dealt with Tuaregs before. They can be sitting under your ass before you know they're there. So keep sharp and keep off the air till I call you."

One by one they responded, acknowledging Dominic's orders. They would do as they were told. Those that had fought the Tuaregs before knew he was right. The serious manner in which they took Dominic's orders had the desired effect on the others who had had no experience with the nomads. All eyes faced out from the salt flat, fingers on the safeties of their weapons though the metal was so hot it was painful to touch. One of the men new to the desert wondered how hot it had to get before the bullets in the magazine would explode.

Dominic saw the glint of silver in the sky before he heard the motors. The plane was making its approach. It rode just above the heat waves, coming straight on. The pilot must have had the salt flat lined up perfectly.

The shape of the aircraft was visible for a minute, then it vanished as it dropped into the heat waves and was lost in the shimmering brightness. Then it was there again. The engines were out of place in the land of silence and desert winds. Landing gear down, the plane was only a hundred feet off the deck, gliding in smoothly. It touched down gently, rubber tires pushing into the salt crust. Flaps full, throttles cut back, it slowed to a near stop, then taxied over to where the Land Rovers waited. The side door was already open.

Dominic climbed into the cab of his vehicle and drove across the salt flat to meet them. The arrivals were out of the plane and off-loading gear when he reached them.

Gus greeted him as he got out of the Land Rover. "Well Dominic, you pretty bastard, where are the girls? I send you to this beach and now you don't have a proper welcome for Uncle Gus. Shame on you."

"Knock it off, Gus, and give the others a hand," Langers barked.

Langers had come from behind the plane followed by Sharif Mamud ibn-Hassani. Dominic brightened up. It was good to see him and the huge German. Mamud wore his usual outfit of jellaba and turban while Langers, like the others, was in battle dress, French camouflage splinter pattern, a Mats-49 slung at his side, full-battle fit. Dominic picked his pack out of the pile and dug out his own uniform. Changing into it made him feel good. It was like the old days, Indochina, Algeria.

Gus did as Langers had ordered and helped the other men with the last of their gear. As soon as the cargo bay was clear Parrish moved out, taxiing to the southernmost end of the strip, pointing his nose into the wind, and taking off without further ceremony. His job was done and now he wanted out. In a few hours he would be drinking cold beer and wondering if the men he took out to the "devil's hammer" would ever be seen again. In the event that they did not make it back, he promised himself to have at least one cold beer in each man's memory.

Sims, their gay British medic, was handing out salt tablets and chiding the men to be careful about insect stings and snake bites.

"Get the gear loaded and let's move out!" Langers ordered. "Dominic, where do we go from here?" He knew that Dominic had made his recon of the area so he let him take over.

Dominic pointed to the west across the desert to where a dark shape rose up seventy miles away. An island in a sea of sand, their destination, Mt. Baguezane.

"We go southwest for about fifty kilometers," he explained, "then follow a wadi back to the north for another two until it turns almost due west. We can stay in the wadi till we are about five or six kilometers from the base of the mountain. Then it gets too rough and we'll have to pull out of it.''

"Good," Carl said. "I like that the wadi will give us some cover. We'll hole up when we get to within five or six kilometers of the base. By then it'll be dark. We'll rest for a while before going on, just to play it safe." To Mamud he queried, "What do you say, old one? Is that the way to go in?''

Stroking his beard between long fingers, Sharif Mamud looked toward the mountain. He had never come to it from exactly this direction. It took only a moment for him to realign his internal compass, then all was clear.

"It's the best way at this time. Once we are near the base of the mountain it will be more clear to me. But we should hope to be near to the southern half of it.''

Dominic referred to his map. "That's where we'll be, near a rock formation that looks like a camel's head.''

Sharif Mamud knew the place. "That will be good.''

"All right then," Carl said. "Let's get to it.''

Sharif Mamud and Carl sat with Dominic in the lead vehicle, putting Gus in the rear to bring up drag. They headed out into the desert, leaving the white death behind them. Langers made them take their time. To hurry in the desert was to invite disaster. If one of the Land Rovers broke down they'd have to abandon it. They would take it easy.

For the first five hours the mountain never seemed to get any closer. Langers knew that it would be near nightfall before they were close enough to feel its presence.

There was little talk from any of the men. Dust coated their faces and lips. It wasn't long before all of them had the long scarves of the Legion wrapped around their faces to keep out the cloying dust. To open your mouth was to dry it out. It was easier to just try and let your body go with the movement of the Land Rover and nod, half-asleep, which would eat up minutes of heavy time.

They came to the wadi formed by the infrequent rains which gathered on Mt. Baguezane, ran off in floods to barely feed the sands, and then vanished, soaked up as if they had never been. But over the centuries the rains had cut away at the kalichi soil.

The wadi was wide enough at most places for two or even three vehicles to drive abreast in it. Boulders appeared more frequently. They had to steer around them, constantly changing gears to navigate through the wadi's maze of twists and turns, soft sand, and chock holes. The Land Rovers did noble duty. As they neared the mountain, the terrain outside the wadi became more rocky. Larger patches of brush and cactus spotted the landscape and inside the gully the going was even rougher. But they were getting closer.

Suddenly Mt. Baguezane loomed ahead of them. Heavy, ominous, it stood out of place. From a distance it had looked smooth and soft. Now it was clear that the mountain was anything but soft. It stood naked, daring them to come to it.

At last they came to where Dominic said they were to stop. Bodies ached. Every muscle had its own special pain. Gratefully the crew stretched legs and arms, twisting their backs to loosen them of the stiffness that had set in. Gus spread his arms out and breathed in deep, thumping his chest.

"By God, a little drive in the country does make one feel just marvelous."

He was roundly cursed by the rest of the party but only under their breaths. Carl felt the same way as the rest. Sometimes Gus could be a real pain in the ass.

"Okay, men," Carl commanded, "we wait here. Cold camp. No fires. Gus, set out a perimeter and see that everyone gets fed and watered. The rest of you stay out of the sun and if you want to lie down, scrape away the top layer of sand. It's so hot it'll pull the moisture out of your body, but underneath the top layer it's cooler. Find cover and rest. Drink your fill but do it slow so you don't get sick. If you fall out you'll be left to get back on your own, and you know what the chance of that is. None!"

CHAPTER ELEVEN

Langers called Sharif Mamud to him. Taking the old man by the arm, he led him to a rocky rise that looked toward Mt. Baguezane.

"We'll start over it in the morning," Langers told him. "The Land Rovers will be sent on ahead. You said it would take two days to make the crossing, but I want to get there before nightfall so I can get a look at the layout. Also, at some place on the way when we come across a setup similar to Sunni Ali's camp, I want to run a rehearsal with the men."

Sharif Mamud clasped his arms together. "It grows cold, al-Kattel. The chill of the night sets deep into the bones, but it is a good cold. You know this is not an easy thing for me to do. In many ways my heart is with Sunni Ali and his desires. It is a pleasant dream, a fantasy most inviting. But it is only a dream, He cannot win. If I thought for one moment that he had a real chance to succeed, I would not be here with you. I would be with him. I do this only to save lives and pain. Yet it is most hard to give up the past and even harder to lose one's dreams."

Carl looked to the mountain. His voice distant he said, "I know, my friend, what it is to lose dreams. More than you would believe, I know."

Sharif Mamud watched the face of his companion. Softly he touched the scar-faced man's arm. "Yes, I do think you understand."

Gus had sent out the sentries, Stachel and Sims taking first watch. The temperature was dropping quickly. It would be a long, cold night but Carl had known nights longer and colder. He would survive.

Roman and Dominic had drawn the last watch. At first light they roused the rest of the team. Carl gave permission for a hot meal to be fixed if they used the sterno stove. If anyone was watching, in a few minutes the movements of the Land Rovers pulling out would give their position away anyway, so it didn't make much difference.

When they finished eating he ordered them to sterilize the area. All trash was to be put in the Land Rovers and any sign of their night in the wadi to be erased as much as possible. It was, of course, impossible to completely wipe out their presence, but he didn't want to give anything away about their numbers if he didn't have to.

When they cleaned up he told them: "Get out the gear and divide up the heavy stuff. Everyone shares the load. Weapons on safety till I say otherwise. I don't want any accidental shots going off this early in the game."

This was the quiet time, when weapons and ammo were distributed. Jokes stopped as the tools of battle were put into their new master's hands: grenades, clips of ammo, magazines, battle dressings, and rations. Roman took the 30 cal light machine gun with the shoulder stock and bipod, with Abdul acting as his loader. Between them they divided up the machine gun ammo. They were ready now, waiting for the word from Langers.

"All right, this is how it plays. Sims, I want you, Graves, and Felix to take the Land Rovers and head back north around Baguezane." On their map he pointed to the location he wanted them to reach. "I want you to be at this point in Mt. Baguezane, where the letter 'E' is on the map. We'll make radio contact with you when we've got the hostages and it's time to move out. We'll need you to be on time if we're going to break contact with the Tuaregs and make it to the LZ where Parrish is to pick us up. Stay away from anyone you see—nomads, goatherds, tourists. Don't let anybody get close to you. If Sunni Ali has word about our geological expedition, I don't want him to get a different count on the number of men involved with it. He's probably going to be suspicious anyway if he just hears of a couple of ferengi vehicles roaming around the desert within a hundred miles of him. I would be."

Sims interjected, "Wouldn't it be best, love, if I went with the main party? You might have need of my tender touch, wouldn't you now?''

Carl shook his head. "No. I want you with the Land Rovers. I told you before that anyone who couldn't keep up was dead meat. Any minor injuries we'll be able to deal with. Anything major and you wouldn't have time to treat it anyway. I want you where I know you'll be able to help after we make the raid.''

Sims pouted a bit. "Well, if that's the way you want it, love, then that's the way it'll be. But do try to get as many back to me as possible. I have grown attached to you bleeding rotters just a bit, you know?''

Carl walked them over to the Land Rovers.

"We'll be on the radios at 1200 hours and again at 1800 hours every day. Captain Parrish will choose one or the other of those times to make a radio link to you. So keep your ears on them. In the mountains we might have some trouble with communication but don't worry about it. Once we're on the western slope we should have no problems. However, if by the fourth night you don't hear from us, *get out*. Make your way back to Fort Laperrine or into Mali.''

Felix showed no sign of emotion. If anything he felt a touch of relief. He knew that he, Graves, and Sims had the best chance of living out the week, and one did not question providence when it worked in your favor.

A wind was starting to rise. Carl looked to the south. "Good, that will help cover our tracks and those of the Land Rovers. That's it. Get going and good luck.''

Sims led the way in the head vehicle. It was going to be a long drive. The rest of the team watched the Land Rovers disappear from sight, then turned to look toward Mt. Baguezane.

''Get your gear on,'' Carl instructed. ''From this time on there will be patrol discipline. No smoking because someone will leave butts lying around. If you eat, put the wrappings back in your packs. Leave nothing on the ground, and stay out of your canteens. We'll all drink at the same time and the same amount. Sharif Mamud says there are water holes up there, but no one knows for certain. If you run out then you go dry, for I'll let no man give another any from his share—think about it. Now let's form up, we have a lot of distance to cover.''

He turned things over to Sharif Mamud who took point, taking the first steps to guide them through the labyrinths of gullies, canyons, and crevices that was Mt. Baguezane. They weren't much as far as numbers went: ten men in single file. They began the long climb to the pass which Sharif Mamud said waited for them at the 7,000-foot level.

Once they hit the trail Sharif Mamud wanted, Carl had him point out the way. Then he moved back from the point and turned it over to Dominic. As they climbed Dominic set a good pace, not too fast not too slow. Carl tried to get a feel for their rate of movement. They probably would be on the way down before their legs got used to the strain.

After an hour's climb Langers stopped on a cliff, looking back down to the desert. Heat waves rose and wavered as far as the eye could see. Sand dunes were broken by reefs of stone beds worn smooth by the passing of centuries. Squinting his eyes, miles away he saw a thin tendril of dust rising into the air, then another, and another. The Land Rovers, most likely.

After the first hour they had switched off on point, giving each a chance to set the pace. Breathing was heavy and hard. Even as they climbed it didn't seem any cooler. The rocks were hot enough to cook meat on. Thin patches of scrub brush poked out between granite boulders, pathetically seeking enough moisture to sustain life.

Sharif Mamud held up better than most of the others. His body was acclimated to the desert heat. Steadily and with sure feet he climbed silently now as they moved up the narrow trails to the pass. The rest of them were quiet except for gasps of labored breathing. Flies had come to buzz over them, swarming on their backs to suck at the salty sweat that had begun to turn their tunics white, adding a lighter pattern to the brown and green camouflage.

All breaks were set by Sharif Mamud. Only he knew how long it would actually take to reach their kickoff point. The team did well, no grumbling, no bitching; they had settled in. Once more

Monpelier had proved his accurate judgment of men. They all helped each other, giving someone a hand or taking a load from another over the rough spots.

At midday they rested, taking shelter in the shade of sun-splintered boulders. They would wait now for a few hours and try to sleep. Most put scarves around their faces, leaving only their eyes uncovered. Exposed skin drew the flies.

Sharif Mamud squatted on his haunches, rocking back and forth for a time as though trying to reconcile great problems. It was in these lands that the great philosophers and prophets of the Moslem world had been inspired. Here where the supernatural *djinns* of the desert and God were always close at hand, to touch them one had only to reach out and feel the wind.

When the sun began its descent they moved once more. Loads became heavier with each kilometer. With the dark Sharif Mamud took the lead again, guiding the way through gullies and canyons that he had not seen in forty years. They were still fresh in his mind and here nothing had changed. They would march all night. It would be easier to keep warm that way and once they set foot on Baguezane, Carl would permit no fires. When they stopped it would be a cold camp.

Near midnight Mamud called a halt. Gratefully men slid to the earth, easing the pack straps from sore shoulders. Boots were taken off and feet rubbed to rid them of the thousands of tiny grains of sand that had worked their way inside. Canteens were drunk from sparingly, though each man wanted to open his throat and let the water flow. Some opened cans of fruit to suck at the sweetness of tinned peaches or pears.

Sharif Mamud ate nothing and only once had Carl seen him take a small drink of water. He knew it was the barren rocks and dry winds which fed something deep inside the old man and gave him strength. Carl came to sit beside him while Egon and Gus stood watch, one at each end of the trail.

Sharif Mamud stared into the distance. His nostrils flared, breathing in the cool air.

"What do you see in the night, old one?"

Mamud didn't move.

"I see the past and the present. I see times yet to come when my people will be lost. Bit by bit they will change, becoming less and less until they are no more."

Carl knew he was talking about their souls. This, the desert, was the true home of his Bedouin people.

Resting his back against the smooth hardness of a boulder, Sharif Mamud spoke softly. "Why do you do this, al-Kattel? I know that it is not for gold. I have read your eyes too many times in the past to believe that."

Carl scratched at the dirt with a fingernail. "Sharif Mamud, my friend. Has it not been written that one has no control over the path his steps will take? All has been written long before we drew our first breath or nursed at our mother's breast. I am no more than what has been ordained for me and do not control it. I am what God has made me. *In sha' Allah!*''

Mamud nodded his head in understanding. ''As you have said, all is in the hands of God. Yet that troubles me. If it is so, then why do we attempt to change anything? Ah, I am ready for paradise. The questions of this life plague me more with each passing year. When one loses the passions of youth, the disease of thinking too much takes over.'' He paused. ''Will you kill Sunni Ali, my friend?''

Carl shrugged his shoulders. ''That depends on circumstances. I have no orders to that effect. If we could, I would prefer not to kill anyone. But I wouldn't bet on that happening, and from what little we know of Sunni Ali, I think that it will be very hard not to kill him. He may demand it.''

Mamud understood. ''Yes, there is a time to die. If one lives on dreams then what has one to live for when the dreams are dead? For such a one it is best that he go with his dreams. It would be a kindness.''

Carl rose to make the rounds. ''Rest now for a time. We still have a long way to go before that judgment has to be made. Rest well. I will be close by if you need me.''

He left Sharif Mamud in the same position as he had found him. He had the feeling that the old man had not only been talking about Sunni Ali; he had been speaking of his own dreams. Even in that Carl wished him well, for indeed there was time to die. For most men, anyway . . . .

Leaving the camp behind, Carl climbed to the edge of a granite outcrop. From there he could look out over the endless wasteland stretching to forever. Forever . . . How long was that? For some it was minutes, for others, eternity. But all things must end. He believed that, though at times he had difficulty believing that about himself.

Cold winds washed over him, causing ripples over and through the myriad scars on his body. Closing his eyes he stood and swayed back and forth on the lip of the ridge. He almost let himself fall forward, but it would have done no good. Death was denied him now as it had been for two thousand years.

Two thousand years . . . From the time of Golgotha to now he, Casca Rufio Longinus, had marched and fought under the banners of innumerable armies and kings. Time and again he had been slave and soldier, and more often a slave to his own weaknesses. He was trapped in the pattern of his past and there was no escape. He was on the endless wheel which the ancient sage Shiu Lao had spoken of on the galley heading for Rome, the great wheel of eternity which turned upon itself, always repeating never-ending cycles.

The worst were the dreams. For weeks at a time

he would fear sleep and the dreams that came with it. The lost faces, the lost loves. Futile to question, useless to fight against, he would go on as he always had, even though for him there was no purpose in doing so.

From the south the winds howled through the clefts and cracks of the massif. His mind asked, as it had a thousand times past, ''When can I rest?'' And the winds replied as always, ''When we meet again . . . .''

CHAPTER TWELVE

Before dawn Langers roused his crew.

"Let's do it. Time to move out." There were the expected groans of frustration from the men, whose tired bodies were not yet ready to rise. Eyes were sticky, legs and arms stiff.

In a couple of hours it would be time to try and contact Sims and his group. He hadn't been able to raise them at the last call. That didn't bother him a great deal; one call missed was no problem. If they missed the next one, however, he would start to be concerned.

Carl had Abdul take the point with Mamud behind him, then he was next and the rest trailed single file with Gus bringing up drag.

It was a little after 0700 hours when Mamud called a halt. "We are almost at the pass. From there it will be downhill."

Welcome words. "All right, Dominic. Send out sentries, then take a break and eat if you want to." Rations were broken out.

As they ate, Mamud spread his jacket on the earth to serve as a prayer rug and faced toward Mecca. The rest stopped their chewing and talking. The relationship between an old man and his god were to be respected, even by those who didn't believe or understand.

Their passing was observed mainly by mottled gekko lizards crawling on the rocks to sun themselves before the heat of the day forced them back into the shade. They made one stop at midday by a spring with cool water bubbling out from the mountain depths. There they waited for an hour, luxuriating in the incredible sensation of a cold wet rag on the face.

Langers kept an eye out for any signs of weakness. When you laid off for a while it normally took a few days to get your legs back. His group seemed to be doing well enough. The loads were evenly distributed, so no one could bitch much about that.

Mamud came to Langers after his prayers. He had scouted the countryside. "I have found a place similar to the camp of Sunni Ali. If you wish to do a rehearsal it will have to be now, for soon we will be too close to the camp to do so."

He led Carl over a hill to where they looked down into a shallow gorge. Mamud was right; it was a good spot, with the exception of the missing caves. But there was no way to rehearse that part anyway.

"Good, my friend. Go and get the others. This will do just fine," Carl said.

It took about fifteen minutes before Mamud returned. Carl had gone down into the gorge to look at the layout, comparing its features with those from the photos. When the men arrived he walked them around, pointing out what didn't belong and what did. Step by step he walked them through their jobs. Using a large boulder as the entrance of the caves, he guessed what the placement of sentries would be.

Then the first rehearsal commenced, dry fire naturally. They went through the escape using a fire team's maneuver for cover, then leapfrogged back. They went through it at a quarter of the actual speed at first, then finally at full speed. Three more times they ran through the exercise until at last Carl was satisfied. It was less than perfect. There would have to be some modifications made once they were on site and got a look at the real thing. But it was important to get the men to move together, to let them get the feel of each other and what was going to be required of them.

Everyone was sweat-soaked and pale-faced by the time the exercise was over. But they felt good, more comfortable. At least now they had a rough idea of what was to go down.

Gus wiped sweat from his brow with a bear-sized paw. "God, what I wouldn't give for a liter or two of good Russian vodka. You know, just a taste to cut the dust from my sensitive palate!"

"All right, gentlemen," Carl announced, "you can take a break now. But remember, when we hit we have to move fast and sure. There won't be time for us to screw around any. As soon as we have the hostages, we bug out. Give each other as much cover as you can and maybe we'll come out of this clean. If not, you know the score. Anyone that goes down and can't move under his own power is shit out of luck. So be careful, but not too careful."

Egon asked Gus dryly, "Is he always so cheerful?"

Gus grunted an affirmative reply. "Yes, but I'll tell you this. He will not leave anyone behind if there is any way at all to get him out."

Egon sighed as he rubbed his aching feet. "Well, that's something anyway."

An hour before sunfall Sharif Mamud told them to hole up in a cleft in the rocks. He wanted to go on ahead to the camp. Sunni Ali was not far now and there would be sentries set.

"Do you want anyone to go with you?" Carl asked him.

"No. I would prefer to go alone. I do not wish to sound officious, but I do make less noise moving than you and your men do with all of your equipment."

Carl thought they had been pretty quiet, but he conceded. "All right, Mamud, as you wish. We'll wait here."

Gus sat in the shade, leaned back, eyes half-closed. At first Carl thought he was mumbling to himself, till he caught the words. Gus was singing, *"Vor die kaserne, vor die grossen tur,"* the old soldier's song of Lilli Marlene. That meant Gustaf was content, though it did seem to upset the lizards, who scuttled for cover at the first off note. Gus just dismissed them as unappreciative critics.

It was fully dark before Sharif Mamud returned to squat beside Langers.

"I have seen the camp. Sunni Ali has it well guarded with several men at the entrance to the caves and more spread out around it in the rocks. They do not seem to be overly alert. Here, let me show you." On the hard-packed earth, with his fingernail, Mamud drew a map of the layout of the camp and where he had seen sentries placed.

"It is as Monpelier said. I would estimate forty to fifty men in the immediate vicinity, but most of those are camped by a spring half a kilometer away. If we can remove the sentries without alerting the others, then we will have a chance of getting in and out. I heard some of the Tuaregs speaking. The hostages are there."

Carl thought about what Mamud had said. The layout wasn't very good. It meant he had to break his men up in order to have any cover fire at all. It wouldn't leave him much to hit the tunnels with and there was no telling what they'd run into inside them. He gave the men around him the layout, described his plan of action, then said, ''If anyone has any suggestions I'm ready to listen.''

They looked at each other, shrugged their shoulders, and shook their head in the negative.

''All right then, that's the way we'll play it. I know it looks tough but I can't think of any other way to do it. I'll give each of you your assignment and we'll move into position an hour before dawn. Till then get what rest you can. Tomorrow promises to be a bit rough.

''Gus, keep an eye on things. I'm going with Mamud for a while. I want to take a look-see at a trail he told me about that we may want to use when we make our break.''

Gus grunted agreeably as he opened a can of spaghetti.

Sharif Mamud led the way, taking Langers down to where a trail branched, one fork going back the way they had come and another leading north and south.

''Have you been on the northern path before, Mamud?''

''Yes, it will take us north for about ten kilometers, then we can cut back to the west and leave the mountain. It will bring us out near to where you want the Land Rovers to meet us.''

Sims wiped the dust off his face and hands with a damp rag. God! This was what he bloody well hated the most. It was so dirty. Unsanitary. However, in spite of the best that nature could do to deter the team of Land Rovers—snakes, sandstorms, gullies, and fields of boulders—they were where they were supposed to be. He hoped that the others hadn't had any difficulties in making the crossing.

He almost wished he'd gone with them. He'd had about enough of the Land Rover jerking his backside out of kilter at every hole and rock it came into contact with. The shocks were about gone. Also, it had been a bit lonely. He was always known as the sociable type. The long ride by himself was a bit depressing. But it had to be done and he was a good sort who would not bother the other chaps with his unhappiness.

The moon was out bright and clear. It was time for his check-in call. Turning on the radio Sims waited. At precisely midnight it came in, clear as a bell. He was using Dominic's former call sign, Gold.

"Right'o Silver. I read you quite clear. Yes, we are on site and in position." Pause. "Very good, sir. We will be ready. Best of luck and do take care, hear?"

Calling Graves and Felix over to him, he told them, "It's going down in the morning, chappies, so better fag out for a couple of hours. We will have a bit of a way to go but I don't want to move out till there's more light. We can't take a chance on losing one of the Land Rovers now, can we?"

Langers's eyes came open. His mental clock

was working. Stiff, he rose and stretched out. Gus was watching him. ''About that time, Herr Feldwebel?''

''Yes, get 'em up.''

Gus roused the rest of the team. They gathered around Carl.

''Let's do this right, men. I don't want anything on you that makes noise. Tape everything down. Don't dump any water from your canteens though. We'll leave them, our packs, and the radio where we'll pick them up on the way out. Once we're ready to make the hit, I don't want you to have anything on you but your weapons. Kitchner, I want you on the mortar. You'll have plenty of time to gauge your distance so I don't want many misses. We're going to need you for cover when we make our getaway. Once that is done you'll destroy the tube, so use all the rounds you can. When we take out the sentries I'll use myself, Dominic, and Egon.''

Sharif Mamud interrupted. ''It would be best if I were also included in case we are spotted. My being able to speak the language might buy us a few seconds.''

Langers would have preferred to leave him out of it, but he did need all the help he could get. ''All right, Mamud. You work with Dominic. At this time I want the silencers put on. If we run into any unexpected visitors going down the trail, let them do the shooting. No noise, that is vital!''

Kitchner asked, "What about the Land Rovers, sir? Will they be on time?"

"Yes. I spoke with Sims at midnight. They'll be ready and where we want them. Don't worry about them. Just do your job and everything will work out. Once more I'm going to tell you: Be careful and don't take chances. A bad hit and you're out of the game forever. Unless you'd prefer that we leave that to the Tuaregs." From the expressions on their faces he knew there wasn't anyone who preferred that fate to a quick clean death.

"All right. You have ten minutes to get ready, then we go."

They were silent enough now to please even Sharif Mamud. Keeping to the shadows, they moved down the trail. At the junction where the trail branched off Langers had them stow their excess gear. He gave them one last break. From here it was only one more kilometer to the caves. He wanted them rested.

Mamud went ahead a hundred meters. His eyes and ears might have been old but they were still the sharpest there. Carl came next. The men spread out with ten meters between each of them. In case of ambush they wouldn't be bunched up.

They reached a ring of boulders from where they could look down on Sunni Ali's camp. It was almost time. Mamud pointed out the guards, dark shadows in desert robes. Carl called Egon,

Dominic, and Mamud to him and gave them their targets, then indicated to Kitchner where he was to set up the mortar. The men stacked the mortar shells they'd been carrying beside the tube. Kitchner took a long look at the target area, making mental calculations on the angle and the number of charges to use for propellant.

He gave Langers a thumbs-up sign. "Piece of cake, sir."

Weapons were given one last check-over. The time to move was now. They began their descent to the caves.

CHAPTER THIRTEEN

Sunni Ali was taking his ease in his tent; the caves were too confining. He sat cross-legged on cushions of woven camel hair, sipping coffee with seeds of cardomon added for spice. Pungent, aromatic, the thick brew soothed his thoughts.

Things were going well. He had received a communication from his agent: St. Johns was ready to comply with his demands. He asked only for time to work out the details of transport, a difficulty which Ali understood. Shipping large quantities of weaponry from one continent to another would require some planning. He had no doubt that St. Johns could accomplish the task. The old bandit had been doing exactly that since the end of World War I.

Allah had been good to Sunni Ali, giving into his hands the one thing which St. Johns valued more than his wealth—his son. For one such as he, this son was the continuation of his name, his only link to immortality—a powerful inducement to make a recalcitrant personality see reason. If there were no unforeseen difficulties, Sunni Ali estimated that he should receive the first shipment of arms in no more than five weeks.

He was glad that he did not have to live up to his threat to dismember the boy and his wife one piece at a time. He had no use for senseless cruelty and gained no pleasure from it. Sadism was a weakness of the spirit, something he would not tolerate in himself. He sipped his brew, smacking his lips over it. That he would have done so if it had been required, there was no doubt. But he took satisfaction in the thought that he would not have enjoyed it.

Once he had his weapons he would live up to his end of the bargain and release the hostages unharmed. He would have no further use for them. He also wanted the world to know that Sunni Ali was a man of his word. A man of honor. That was important. All must know that he would do exactly as he said. There was nothing like the truth; it was the sharpest of swords. A sword which could set his people free or slice the throats of those who tried to keep him from fulfilling his destiny.

Outside he could hear the whinny of horses and the movement of his men around their campfires. Good, familiar sounds. Natural sounds. In the shadow of the massif the winds were softened, giving them shelter from the whirling sand devils of the open desert.

Five weeks. Then he would send out his messengers to all the tribes, calling them to rally with him in his *jihad,* his holy war aginst those who would take their heritage from them. In time they would come to him. They would have to or they would die. In a war such as he planned there was no place for sentiment. Only the true, the righteous, deserved to survive. Those who opposed him must fall. There was no other way. *Allah akbar!* God is great!

It was with a deep feeling of satisfaction that Sunni Ali lay down upon the pallet which served as his bed. He would sleep well this night. For the stars were in their proper course and each coming dawn brought him closer to fulfillment. All was well.

Dominic felt his temples begin to pound, his palms to sweat, his heart to race. Anticipation. God, it felt good. For the first time in months he felt alive. Holding his knife close to his side, he crawled closer and closer, taking his time. There was no need to rush things now. The pace had settled into a pattern. Like sex, it should not be rushed or it would be spoiled. He knew the rest of the team was with him though they couldn't be seen. His total concentration was on what he was to do in the next few moments.

Turning his head at a whisper of the night wind, the sentry's eyes ran over the dark. Then he turned back to watch the campfire where his brothers sat about the burning coals. Soon it would be his turn to sit by the fires and listen to the rhythmic pulse of the *allun* as each of the warriors took their turn at telling stories.

Dominic slid closer, letting his mind project itself forward. He knew beforehand every move the Tuareg would make.

Above him Roman waited with Abdul, the Sudanese. He placed the light machine gun in the best position for covering fire. They had the hard part, the waiting. Not being able to do anything but wait for the others to move.

Gus kept close to Carl's heels. They had to wait also. This was Dominic's work. They knew, from the months during the siege of Dien Bien Phu when time and again they had gone out into the Viet Minh positions, that Dominic was the best, the most dependable. The sentry had to be taken out silently if they were to get inside the caves before the Tuaregs knew of their presence, and such a job required their best man.

The sentry adjusted the Mauser rifle on his shoulder. He did not like this business of standing watch but Sunni Ali ordered it, so it would be done. He knew that no harm would come to them at this place, far from the power of the feringi. If anyone had approached, their outlying scouts would have let them know hours before they could get to the caves. But *in sha' Allah*, God's will. He reconciled himself to the lonely, boring hours of standing watch.

His boredom came to a sudden halt. Dominic moved. Gathering his legs under him, he came to within ten feet of his quarry. He took a deep breath and held it in, compressing the air down deep inside his abdomen. He moved again, left hand leading. The Tuareg's back was inches away. Dominic's hand slid around, going for the sentry's throat. It missed and hit the mouth. Instantly the Tuareg bit down hard. Dominic forced his hand more solidly against the man's mouth to stifle any outcry as his knife came down at the junction of neck and collarbone, heading for the carotid artery. The Tuareg tried to scream as he felt the steel turn and twist in his neck as it searched for the major artery that sent blood to the brain. It found it. The knife punctured, then severed the thick vessel, probing deeper as the blade cut a three-inch opening in the upper lobe of the right lung. The Tuareg began to bleed, blood pouring out in gouts and spurts as Dominic held him close. He desperately wanted to cry out a warning. Then he wanted to plead for mercy but knew it was too late. He was dying and there was nothing on this earth that could save him. His last thoughts were *La ilah illa' Allah: Muhammad rasul Allah*. There is no god but Allah: Mohammed is His prophet.

Dominic let the body slide easily to the earth, then grabbed it by its robes and dragged it behind the boulder to where Sharif Mamud waited. Swiftly the old man put on the Tuareg's jellaba, wrapping the veil over his face to leave only his eyes uncovered. Disguise intact, Mamud took the

Tuareg's place as Dominic slid back into the shadows.

Squatting behind a patch of brush, Carl waited for the next victim to come near. The sentry was in the most exposed position. He patrolled the fringe of the light cast by the campfire. Carl would have to be quick and silent. Twice the sentry passed him but each time there were too many eyes from the campfire looking his way. It was hard to get set, be ready, then not be able to move, only to have to wait again. The man came close. Then from the cave came a call. Automatically all eyes turned to the entrance. Carl moved, rising up from the patch of brush which concealed him. His hand grasped the Tuareg's throat and he squeezed his fingers, going deep into the cartilage of the esophagus, crushing it as he dragged the body back into the shadows. Another change of clothing and Egon had taken the Tuareg's place. By the time all eyes had returned to the campfire, Carl had two men in critical positions, one on each side of the cave entrance. It was almost time.

Carl clicked his fingers once, then again. Sharif Mamud moved closer to the ring of men sitting and nodding to the beat of the skin drum. Egon did the same. At their waists their weapons were held in the horizontal position, barrels pointing casually forward. Their Mats-49s had longer snouts than usual. Silencers. Twenty feet away, then ten, Sharif Mamud came near the fire, A man turned to him, his lips forming a question. The question

was never spoken. He died too quickly. Sharif
Mamud's first burst took out three men instantly,
pumping fifteen subsonic 9mm's into their
bodies. Less than a heartbeat behind him came
Egon's burst of fire, cutting down the others,
who had no opportunity this time to make their
peace with God. The only sound from the submachine guns was that of the bolts slapping back
and forth. Eight men died. Carl and the rest of the
team emerged from the shadows, leaving Egon
and Sharif Mamud to guard the cave entrance.

Carl moved out into the open. From behind him
came the rest of the team. Weapons at the ready,
they hit the entrance to the cave. As they moved
inside Sharif Mamud and Egon dragged the dead
away from the campfire into the dark, then took
up positions on each side of the mouth of the cave.

Following Mamud's directions they split into
two units where the cave mouth separated. Carl
and Gus went to the left while Dominic and Foche
took the tunnel to the right. They ran in a crouch.
Two men lay on their sides, blankets about them.
Carl passed them by, leaving them to Gus and the
others. Swift cuts taking less than five seconds
and Gus was on Carl's heels, putting his knife
back into its sheath as he ran.

Ahead of Carl was a brighter guiding light. He
slowed to a halt. Gus nearly knocked him down
coming to a stop. Carl listened. Voices speaking
Tamahaq. Then he heard one in English ask for
something. He couldn't make out what it wanted,

but the voice was definitely that of a girl. He
pointed to the other side of the tunnel, indicating
to Gus and one other to move over there. They
waited a moment, then began to move closer to
the light.

Carl knew the others could sense the timing.
They didn't have to be told. Instincts were working. He knew that each of them took a breath at the
same moment he did. They burst into the light,
fingers taking up trigger slack to the width of a
hair. They each picked out their targets.

Dark eyes had little time to register alarm before bullets began smashing into faces and bodies.
In the cavern the sound was deafening as the
submachine guns roared and jerked. Carl moved
to his left, keeping the wall to his back.

The girl and her husband were at the far end on
his side. There was only one way out. "Lie down
and don't move!" he screamed at them over the
deafening echoes of gunfire. They did as they
were ordered. Face down, hands over their heads,
they lay still. Only one Tuareg managed to get off
a wild shot that clipped Gus on the ear, taking with
it a dime size plug. The rest went down.

Jumping over bodies Carl grabbed the girl by
her arm and jerked her to her feet, then did the
same to the boy. "Get up and move. Stay behind
me and do as I say."

He ran back to the cavern entrance, telling Gus,
"You bring up drag."

They moved back out. Reverberations echoing through the tunnels told Carl the other group had made contact. Probably their shots had set off the Tuaregs. If the other group wasn't pinned down, they would be doing as he had ordered and heading back to the entrance where Egon and Sharif Mamud were on guard. Cries of pain came with the gunfire. Curses in Arabic, Tamahaq, and French 'were all mixed together. He knew men were dying and could only hope that they weren't his.

Sharif Mamud and Egon heard the noise. Moving out of the light they knelt down, recognizing the sound of gunfire coming from inside the cave. As muted as it was, it would bring more warriors.

Roman and Abdul strained their eyes against the dark. They could hear voices. They couldn't understand them but they knew that men were coming. Roman adjusted the metal shoulder stock more securely. Abdul held the shiny brass belt of linked ammo delicately in his hand, ready to move with Roman and keep the belt feeding smoothly, his fingers ready to feel for any twist in it that could cause a stoppage.

Inside the cave a major firefight had started. Dominic had run into the section of tunnel used as sleeping quarters for Sunni Ali's guards. These were the men Ali had trained personally. Even though Dominic and Foche had gotten off the first shots, the Tuaregs responded quickly. Foche went down. Gut shot. Dominic changed magazines lying down along the tunnel as sparks ricocheted off the stone walls.

Dominic looked down at Foche. Blood was coming from his stomach and his back. He was a goner. Foche knew it too. Blood bubbling between his lips, he choked out, "Well, get on with it. You know what has to be done. You wouldn't leave me alive for them to play with, would you?" He coughed, a piece of torn flesh from his stomach coming up to his mouth. He spat the bloody clot out and looked up, waiting. Dominic knew he was right. He glanced down the tunnel. Men were gathering there and there was no way he could hold them by himself. Without any hesitation or warning he pointed his submachine gun down and blew the top of Foche's head off. Instant death, freedom from pain.

Dominic moved back taking Foche's weapon with him. Now he was just trying to keep them off his back as he fought his way to the entrance of the cave. At the junction he met with Carl and Gus. He answered the unspoken question.

"Foche is dead."

Sparks ricocheted off granite walls. Sparkles of light from both sides searched for soft tissue to enter. The superior firepower of the raiders gave them an advantage. Changing magazines as fast they could, barrels were already heating up to a red glow in the dark.

"Grenades by series!" Carl commanded.

Pins were pulled and the bombs were tossed into the dark as far as they were capable of throwing them. Carl used the grenades as a delaying tactic. Throw a couple, then retreat, throw a couple, then retreat. They leapfrogged back to the entrance of the caves.

The voices outside had come together in a mass. Cries of anger and confusion were closer. Egon and Mamud could hear them clearly. The dull thumps of the grenades in the tunnel told them they were about to get into deep shit. If the Tuaregs boxed them in at the mouth of the cave they would be trapped.

Roman's mouth grew dry and sticky. He looked at Abdul, his black face oily in the dark. They knew that their waiting for action was about to end. Abdul smiled gently at the Spaniard as if to say, "It is in the hands of God."

Sunni Ali heard the muted gunfire. Rising from his bed he rushed out of his tent, calling his men to him. He had no doubt as to what was taking place. From their slumbers confused men gathered clutching their weapons.

"To the caves!" he cried. "They are after my hostages. Go! Run! They must be stopped."

Tuaregs swarmed in the dark running, Sunni Ali whipping them on. This was no time for tactics. He didn't care if his men ran into an ambush as long as they slowed up the raiders. He yelled to his senior radio operator, "Reach all you can.

Have them on alert and ready to ride!'' Then he raced after his men, jacking a round into the chamber of his SMG. He was only fifteen seconds behind them.

The first ragged group of eleven Tuaregs entered the light of the campfire. Roman took up the slack. Between the rapid fire of the machine gun and the Mats-49s of Sharif Mamud and Egon, they all went down.

Carl came out of the cave dragging the girl behind him. Her husband bent over to take a weapon from a dead Tuareg. Carl saw. A good sigh this, the young man was ready to fight. Turning the hostages over to Egon and Sharif Mamud he told them, ''Get them away. We'll slow things up here.'' Sharif Mamud led the way past Roman and Abdul, taking them into the dark and removing their Tuareg robes as they went.

Carl gave the rest of the team their orders. ''Into the shadows by Roman. Form a perimeter. Let the main body get into the light by the cave. Wait for my orders to fire.'' He knew it wasn't likely that the next body of Tuaregs to reach them would take off blindly into the dark. They would wait for someone in authority to tell them what to do.

Carl could hear them coming. ''Get grenades ready and pass the word to the others,'' he whispered to Gus. Pins were straightened out and the small bombs set where they were easy to reach.

Sunni Ali came to the entrance of the cave. He didn't have to go inside. He knew his captives were gone. The bodies of the dead did not concern him. What he wanted to know was which way had they gone and how many were there. To his men he cried out, "Spread out and search for their trail!"

Carl couldn't let them do that. He sighted on the man giving the orders and took up the trigger slack. As the last thousandth of an inch was reached, a Tuareg warrior ran in front of his leader and took five rounds meant for Sunni Ali. Carl cursed his luck. When he fired, the rest of the team came in with rapid fire, no fancy shooting. It didn't matter whether what they hit was killed or wounded as long as it stopped them from being able to follow.

"Grenades. Now!"

While the bombs were in the air he told Roman and Abdul, "Take your guns and move out. Set up in the canyon where you can give us cover fire at first light. We'll be right behind you."

Confusion was on their side. The rapid fire from the submachine guns gave them an edge they used to its maximum effectiveness. The sole surviving Tuareg moved away from the glow of the campfire.

Sunni Ali burned up two magazines firing at the ring of boulders. He thought he'd hit one. Whoever it was in the rocks, they were good. They had waited for him to be in an exposed position with his men, when most would have just taken their prize and run for it.

To his lieutenants he ordered, ''Take men, spread out, and keep firing. There can't be too many of them.''

Mamud led the way back into the rocks. Then he turned to cover a section of rough ground, leaving a trail which, if they were lucky, the Tuaregs would think they had taken.

''*Let's do it!*'' Carl yelled as loud as he could over the increasing crescendo of gunfire. ''Leap-frog it out by twos and threes.''

The rest of the team was doing good, steady work, giving each other cover as they withdrew. When the first men passed Kitchner he started dropping rounds down the tube. He placed the first rounds on the far side away from Carl and his men, then started walking them in to the front of the cave.

Sunni Ali ran into the mouth of the cave to take cover. He knew the fire wouldn't last long. The one advantage he had was time. The raiders could not stand and fight. They would have to run, and that was when he would catch them. But right now he had to check on his vehicles to see if they had been damaged or destroyed. His men would pick up their trail and stay on them the rest of the night. With dawn he'd know which way to move and have a better idea of how many of the enemy there were to deal with.

With Gus on his heels, Carl was the last to break contact when the mortar rounds started coming in. The Tuareg went into instant panic and confusion. They weren't used to that kind of firepower coming at them. But Carl didn't fool himself by thinking this was the end of it. He knew they had a long way to go.

CHAPTER FOURTEEN

When they reached Kitchner dropping shells down the mortar tube, Carl yelled out, "Pack it up, blow the rest of your ammo, and get gone!"

Kitchner dropped a grenade down the tube, then another by his remaining rounds—no sense in leaving the enemy anything that might be useful—and took off after Langers and Gus.

They pushed it hard for an hour. Contact was broken with the Tuaregs but he knew it wouldn't stay that way long. When dawn came the nomads would be after them.

"Take five," Carl ordered. "Dominic, set out some trip wires on the back trail. The rest of you spread out where you can rest and still see what's going on. Let's not get careless now.

"Egon, get Sims on the radio. Tell him to move out. We'll be at the rendezvous point by 1100 hours and we'll check in again with him at 0900. Then have him relay the info to Monpelier. Got it?" Egon repeated the message, took the radio, and began to send word.

Sunni Ali was relieved to see that at least the

153

raiders had not gotten far enough back in the
tunnels to find his vehicles. They would be
needed shortly, but first he had to do some thinking.

Retiring to his tent, he took from a mahogany
case his own maps of the region. Time and
movement were the keys. Once he had the direction of the enemy's route confirmed, then he'd be
able to plan. Logic was now needed. Eyes poring
over the map, he checked it against his mind and
memory.

The raiders were on foot and had gone back into
the mountain. They must have transport waiting
for them somewhere. Their commander must
know that if they stayed even one day in the area
they would be found. Their job was to get in and
get out as fast as possible with their prize. Therefore they must be heading to a place where they
would be retrieved by either ground transport or
aircraft.

Considering their rate of movement and the
maximum distance they could travel in a given
period of time, and he would give heavy odds that
he was right about the time factor, it was incon-
ceivable that the raiders would plan on spending
more than twenty-four hours in his land. The
options would be severely reduced once he had
their direction confirmed. There could only be so
many places from which to leave the mountain
and reach a site where transport could pick them
up. When they arrived there, Sunni Ali would be

waiting for them with his own armored cars and heavy weapons.

The lone Tuareg moved between the ancient boulders. For a brief moment his eyes rose to the distant horizon. That was his mistake. The trip wire was broken and a grenade blew his left leg off at the knee. Sunni Ali had his direction.

While he was waiting for such information, he had given orders that the Hanamogs and American jeeps be made ready. Their crews stood by. These men he had trained as carefully as the panzer crews had been trained in Germany during the early days of the war. They knew their jobs.

On his map Sunni Ali made a check mark where the boobytrap had exploded. Soon he would have another mark on his map and with each one he would be closer to reclaiming that which was his. His radiomen had been given the order to contact all outposts. They were put on the alert for any ferengi in the area and were told to stop all forms of motor transport. Nothing was to go through or get out.

Sims was pushing it. Three times he'd had to stop and pull one of the Land Rovers out of sand traps. Wiping his goggles clean he stared hatefully at the mass of Mt.Baguezane. The great bloody thing seemed to go on forever. Graves pulled up alongside of him, yelling out through his window, "Hey limey, did you see them?"

Wearily resigned to such verbal abuse, Sims

responded sardonically, "Of course I saw them, you great bleeding clot. Do you think I'm blind? What's bloody more important, I'm sure they saw us also. And if they did, we could be in for a real pisser, what?"

Shifting into low to climb the side of the wadi Graves yelled back, "So what do you say we forgo this bit of pleasantry and try to reach our destination on time?"

Langers had moved to the rear. The explosion of a grenade had been clearly heard. It had echoed off the stones for miles. He wished they'd had more time to leave a false trail or take better efforts to conceal their movements but they didn't.

Mamud joined him. Shading his eyes with a hand, he looked back the way they had come. "They are there and they are getting closer."

Langers nodded. "I know. How are the kids holding up?"

Mamud inclined his head down the trail they were taking. "They are doing well enough. The boy is strong and eager, and the girl has a good heart but her legs are weak."

Carl wasn't too concerned about that. If necessary he would have Gus carry them out on his back.

"I'm getting a bit worried about the time, Sharif. It would be best if we could slow up the pursuit a bit."

Mamud knew what he was thinking, that the time could come very soon when someone would have to stay behind and fight a delaying action so the others could escape. That would, of course, be their last resort. But it was not yet necessary for such a thing to be done. They still had some time left.

He didn't tell Langers he had seen the figure of a man on their trail in the distance and another to their left flanking them. Langers had enough on his mind and there was nothing he could do about it anyway. Both were at least three kilometers away.

Sunni Ali took the lead half-track, which held his radio, and began to move out to the north, flanking the mountain. He had to make a half-circle to reach clear ground before he could straighten out his angle and run parallel. He didn't push it. To rush was to make mistakes.

He had another call from his scouts on Mt. Baguezane. The raiding party was still heading north. They had come across several other boobytraps, but these had been avoided now that they were aware of them. Half an hour later another call came in from one of his scouting parties to the north, and he knew he was correct. Three Land Rovers had been seen heading south. From the route of the Land Rovers, the direction of the raiding party, and the few places at which they would come together, Sunni Ali began to reduce his options one by one.

Moving to the back of the Hanamog, he stood up behind the machine gun mount. An MG-34. It smelled of new oil. For a few minutes his heart sped up. He had a sense of déjà vù, a taste of those great days when they'd first fought the British in Libya. The Afrika Korps had performed brilliantly. Though outnumbered, and with thin supplies, they had pushed the English back across the desert to the borders of Egypt.

It was good to feel the vibrations of the war machine beneath his feet again. To be on the hunt for the best of all game, men. In front of him, scouting in a fan, were his three American jeeps, useful little things which could go almost anywhere, but it was the half-tracks which were his babies. With him were twenty of his best men who, though they wore the robes of the nomad, had the discipline of the Afrika Korps instilled in them. They would follow orders to the end.

It was good: hot wind on his face, clear skies, and a hunt. He was almost thankful to whoever they were that they had come. He needed this kind of challenge to set his blood moving and to test himself. He would meet the challenge head-on.

Carl had not missed the Tuaregs trailing them. He turned to Mamud. "Let's go, old friend. We have a way to travel yet before we can rest."

They trotted till they caught up with the small column. The girl was weakening. It occurred to

Carl for the first time that he had not taken a good look at the couple. Now that he had them, they were less important than before. The girl stumbled. A huge paw helped her gently to her feet. Carl called out to Gus. "If she falls again, carry her."

Carl moved up behind the young woman. She looked over her shoulder at the man who had rescued her and her husband from the cave. Timidly she attempted a smile, which failed. Even under the coating of dust the man's face had a quality to it, a detachment which frightened her somehow. Not that it was threatening; she didn't feel that. It was just . . . something.

Carl passed her, going up to the head of the column. As he did, he looked carefully at each of his men. They were breathing hard. Sweat streaks on their faces had cut through the dust, giving them an aged appearance.

Overhead he saw a pair of hungry vultures riding the air currents. "Not today, if I can help it. You'll have to look elsewhere for food," he remarked.

Mamud went to the point again, guiding the men through the labyrinth of turns. Twice more Langers saw distant figures. This time one of them was on his right flank, standing on a crest. Men to their left, right, and rear. He didn't like that very much at all.

Taking advantage of the fact that he had no one

to avoid, Sunni Ali was able to make good time. Coming to a small plain near the base of the mountain, he called a halt. It was time now to make yet another move on this vast checkerboard.

He took the radio and made calls, sending the signal out to the desert. At his command, bands of men began to converge. From his men on the mountain Sunni Ali knew he had the raiders right where he wanted them. He would keep the pressure on. He gave his people strict orders not to do any shooting unless it looked like the raiders had a chance of making good their escape. The fleeing prisoners were much too valuable. He wouldn't take chances on a stray bullet ending their usefulness to him. No, this was the time to begin channelizing them. He would present enough subtle yet viable obstacles to force them to move in the direction he wanted.

Sims saw them too. He didn't need Graves' nervous finger to point them out. Riders on the horizon. Through his binoculars he saw there were at least twenty mounted men on horses with each party, one coming behind them from the north and the other to the west. They were making no effort to close in. The riders kept their distance, moving steady but unrushed. Sims didn't like it. He wished that he could have taken some evasive moves but there wasn't time. If he was to be at the rendezvous on schedule, he had no choice but to go on. At the 0900 check-in he would tell Langers what was going on. Maybe he would have some strategy that would help.

Carl placed the mike back on its hanger. To the others gathered around him he said flatly, "Looks like we're in for a bit more shit. This Sunni Ali knows his stuff. He's channelizing us. For those of you who haven't noticed, we have had company for the last couple of hours—Tuareg trailing us on three sides, leaving us only one way to go. Now it looks like he's doing the same thing to Sims. He's boxing us in. From here on out it's double-time. Take nothing but ammo and water; drop everything else. Every second counts if we're going to get out of this in one piece. Gus, the girl is your responsibility."

He turned to her husband. "How are you holding up? Can you go the distance? We have another two hours, maybe less, till we're supposed to meet with the Land Rovers. Can you keep up that long?"

"I can make it," the youth assured him. "I know what's waiting for me back there. Just give me something to shoot with. It'll make me feel like I'm doing something, and I do know how to shoot."

Langers liked the way the young St. Johns spoke, and he did have an extra weapon. "Dominic, give him Foche's piece and an extra magazine."

The men around him were beginning to get that

special look of uncertainty around the edges of their eyes. No one liked to run. It was always easier to attack than defend.

CHAPTER FIFTEEN

From his outriders Sunni Ali knew the exact position and direction the Land Rovers were taking. On his map he began to rule out possibilities of escape. Giving it some thought, he tried to figure out what he would do if he was given the assignment the raiders were on.

The most likely choice of options would be for the raiders to meet with the Land Rovers at a given spot and then make it to someplace a plane could set down to fetch them. Checking his map again against his memory of the area, he touched a spot with his fingernail. "It will be here, and I will be waiting for them."

Felix spotted them first, coming out of the rocks. "There they are!" he cried out. Sims had his kit in hand, ready to take care of any wounds.

Langers was in the lead. He waved Sims back. "No time for that shit now. We have company tailing us. Let's get loaded and get out of here. No one is hurt too badly. Mostly just blisters and sunburn."

Under the coating of fine dust it was hard to tell how badly anyone was sunburned. They all looked the same.

"Sims, I want you and the others to keep driving. You know what the ground is like better than we do. Just get us to the LZ. Monpelier did get the signal, didn't he?"

Sims answered him dryly, slightly offended at the implied question of his competence. "Of course I did. And if I have it timed right, they should be over the LZ within minutes of our own arrival."

"Good. Now let's get gone."

Langers put the girl and her husband in the same Land Rover with Gus. The rest of the crew just climbed gratefully into the vehicles wherever there was room. It was with no regrets that they were leaving Baguezane behind them. They'd had enough of the mountain and were quite content to leave it to the lizards, snakes, and vultures.

It looked as though they might have had it made, but Carl still didn't like the feeling of being herded. "Sims, where was the last place you saw riders?"

"Oh, about twenty kilometers from here. They were heading southwest away from me. Probably just a caravan of some sort, though I was a bit concerned for a time. They were the third group I had seen since yesterday. Why, do you think they're trouble?"

Carl leaned his head back against the seat, trying to ignore the jolting of the Land Rover as Sims maneuvered it between, over, and around obstacles.

"I don't know and that's what bothers me," he admitted. "Those Tuaregs should have been more confused, more disoriented. We hit them pretty hard. Caught them with their pants down. But they came back just as hard, and fast, too. Very professional. They didn't act like nomads. They responded like regular army troops, and damned good ones. We were lucky to get out with no more losses. Very lucky."

Closing his eyes he made one last comment. "Try to keep this thing level. I'm going to try and get some shut-eye. Wake me if you see anything or if we get within five kilometers of the LZ."

"Right'o, love. You got it."

Three dust trails marked their passage as they raced across the scrublands to where the plane would come to get them. Somehow it didn't seem possible that all this had started just a short time before. It seemed much longer than that.

Monpelier leaned over between Parrish and Rigsby. "How much longer?"

Parrish checked his watch. "About an hour, give or take five minutes."

Sunni Ali was ready. The timing was nearly

perfect. His horsemen and his vehicles awaited his command. Hidden behind rocks and in wadis, they had camouflaged their positions very carefully, especially so as not to be seen from the air. If the pilot was worth a damn, he would make at least one quick flight over to check out the area. Ali had reason to be satisfied. He had called the progression of the game perfectly. A bit of pressure here, a touch there, nothing too sinister, but it did force them to reveal what he wished to know. That and the process of elimination gave him the location of the landing zone.

He had kept just enough pressure on the raiders to make them believe they had the edge, but not enough to waste any time. They would be anxious to get away. He knew he could have forced the issue at any time, but he wanted to see if he was right. Now the Land Rovers were at the end of what would be the LZ, a lake bed gone dry and baked as hard as concrete. They were at the south end. That meant the plane would come in from the north. Then they would load there, do a turn around, taxi back to the north, and take off into the wind. He would hit them when they began to load and perhaps, if he was lucky, gain a plane in the bargain.

Sunni Ali had given his warriors their orders. As soon as the plane began to throttle, back on the ground they were to shoot for the tires. His half-tracks would block the runway to prevent the possibility of them taking off, while his jeeps and horsemen would take care of the Land Rovers and their crews. Now it was time for just a bit more patience.

"Silver to Copper. Do you read me? Over." Carl was contacting the plane.

"Roger that, Silver. We've got you five by five. What does it look like down there? Over."

The looks of relief were obvious on all faces except those of Gus, Dominic, and Sharif Mamud. They didn't seem to care one way or the other.

"From where we're at it looks clear. The wind is from the south to north, about ten knots with light gusts."

"I read you. We'll make a flyover and orbit the area for a look-see. Then we'll come on in. Be ready to get on. I don't want to waste any time getting our ass out of here. Over and out."

Parrish took the C-47 into a wide spiral, working toward the center. He saw nothing. Moving off a few miles to the north he turned the nose of the plane, put down his landing gear, lowered his flaps, and started coming in. "Should be easy," he said to Rigsby who merely grunted, his usual response.

The wheels touched down, throwing up a stream of dust behind them. Opening the cargo door, Monpelier stood ready with a Browning automatic rifle. This was no time to get sloppy. Most things, if they went wrong, did so at the last moment.

Langers and his party were ready, but Langers had had a bad feeling for the last fifteen minutes. "Gus! Take a couple of men and one of the Land Rovers and circle the strip. Keep an eye out. There's something wrong. I hope it's just my imagination. If everything's okay we'll meet at the far end. Graves, you and Abdul come with me."

Gus had seen Langers's hunches prove right too many times in the past to argue about it. "Check your weapons, put one in the spout if you haven't already. We're going to take a look-see." Obediently they climbed in, weapons out the windows, ready to fire if need be.

They moved out rapidly. Halfway down the LZ they passed the plane. Gus waved at Parrish in the cockpit, then turned the nose of the Land Rover to avoid a rock and saw a flash to his left.

"Oh shit!" If there was an ambush set up, the only thing he could do was try and spring it before the attackers were ready. He headed straight for the spot where he'd seen the brief sparkle of light behind a screen of brush. "Dominic, watch the right front. I saw something."

Sunni Ali saw the Land Rover. No! It was not yet time. He hoped that his men would hold their fire just one more minute. Then it would make no difference.

The sight of the Land Rover coming straight for them was too much for one young Tuareg. This was his first time on an ambush. Fingers sweating, only his eyes showed the fear and anxiety as the rest of his fourteen-year-old face was covered by the folds of his veil. He didn't know the exact moment when his finger took up the last of the trigger slack. His rifle suddenly bucked against his shoulder; he had fired. The back of his father's hand knocking him from his horse told him he had screwed up.

Dominic returned fire with his SMG spraying wildly, not really planning on hitting anything. But it would let the rest of his party know that some shit was going down bad. Gus whipped the wheel around and headed back to the others. Bullets snapped off twigs and branches from the dried brush and several rounds punched holes in the Land Rover.

Ali was furious. There was nothing else to do now but attack.

"Allah akbar!"

His driver turned out of the wadi, crashing out of the covering of brush they had been using for camouflage. The rest of his men moved at the same time. Horses, half-tracks, and jeeps hit the strip, spreading out in a line from the north end to the south.

Langers piled everyone back in the Land Rovers. He stood at the end of the LZ trying to wave Parrish off. Gus came screeching up to him.

"What do we do?" Gus yelled. "A half-track with a machine gun was on an intercept course with the Dakota. Behind it were jeeps and another half-track, and now horsemen are coming out of the brush."

"We have to get the plane back in the air," Langers replied. "If it goes down we're in deep shit. Get it up and we can try for another rendezvous somewhere else."

Parrish saw the small figure at the end of the runway waving him off. From his open cargo door Monpelier was laying down fire, aiming to the rear over the tail at the pursuing line of Tuaregs. Lines of bullets stitched their way up the side of the plane, their holes letting in the desert light. Parrish estimated the amount of ground he had left: no way to take off again. He'd have to turn around. Rigsby opened his window, pulled a 9 mm Browning out from under his seat, and opened fire, knocking a horseman down.

Parrish had to brake to turn and as he did he got his first good look at what was coming after him. "I don't think this is going to be a nice day," he quipped.

Rigsby grunted again and fired off half a clip.

From their end of the landing zone Langers had the Land Rovers move out after the plane to try and keep the Tuaregs away until it was airborne again.

Sunni Ali found himself in line with the plane. With a touch of regret he aimed the MG-34 at the cockpit. Plexiglass exploded and Parrish's face became a red mask. Rigsby tried to regain control of the plane but Parrish's body had draped over the yoke. The Dakota went into a spin, angling over sharply till her left wing tip touched down.

The movement threw Monpelier out the door to hit the dirt, breaking his right leg. Cursing in three tongues at his own stupidity for coming on the flight in the first place, he squatted in the dirt, snatched up his BAR, and tried to blow away the man with the MG-34. He didn't make it. The half-track ran over him, treads crushing his chest to the thickness of a pack of smokes.

When Sunni Ali opened direct fire on the aircraft so did the rest of his men. A tire blew, then thick whisps of black smoke came from the port cowling. Rigsby fought to regain control. He had the plane just about level when the back of his head erupted. Bullets coming through the fuselage flattened out before hitting him. It was just as well. The plane burst into flames only seconds later.

Langers pulled his men away, angling off to the northwest. There was nothing they could do now. Firing from their windows they punched holes in the Tuareg horsemen. Voorhees took a wild round through his temple. Abdul opened the door and dropped him out. All weapons firing, they broke away. All they could do now was run for it. Langers signaled for Sims to take the lead.

It was an hour later before they broke contact with the Tuaregs and stopped to gauge their situation. Graves and Kitchner were done for as was the Land Rover they were riding in, taking a barrage of Tuareg fire miles back. Felix had taken one too, catching a round in his back. When Sims got out of the Land Rover he was limping badly, having to hold onto the Land Rover to support his weight. Blood came from his pants leg and a dark spot was spreading at his waist. Gus was about to punch Dominic playfully in the side and started to make some remark. He never finished it. Dominic's face was pale, lips drawn tight.

"You hit, Dominic?" Gus asked.

Dominic nodded. Under his right arm, from his side, blood was flowing freely. Gently Gus helped him out of the vehicle. Sims limped over with his medic kit. He and Dominic looked at each other. They knew. After treating Dominic, Sims bandaged himself, took a couple of pain pills, and said flatly, "I think someone else should drive and try to take it easy. Up ahead about thirty kilometers is a narrow mountain pass. I do believe we should try and get through it before the bloody madman can have it blocked."

Langers didn't like it at all. He'd seen too many wounds not to know that Sims and Dominic were badly hurt. The Tuaregs had done them good. The plane was gone, its crew was dead. Kicking one of the tires in frustration, he cursed their luck. A thin hiss of steam was coming from one of the Land Rover's radiators. It had been punctured.

There was nothing else to do. "All right, let's load up and try and get some distance between us. Abdul, you take over driving for Sims. I don't know how far this machine is going to go but we can't stop to worry about it. Load up and let's get out of here. Maybe we will make it to the pass."

CHAPTER SIXTEEN

Sims propped his back against a boulder for support. "Listen to me, love. I am the bloody medic, what? I believe that I am the best judge of the current condition of my health. The leg is shattered and I have internal bleeding. Even if there was room, I wouldn't survive the ride back, what with the bumps and all."

Those gathered around him knew he was right. There wasn't really anything that could be said. Sims knew it, too.

"Right then, this is how it shall be done," he continued. "I will wait here with one of the machine guns and do a bit of stitching. If nothing else it will buy you a bit more time."

Silently Roman placed his weapon beside the medic, laying several ammo belts where they'd be easy to reach. Sims nodded casually.

Langers looked over his survivors, then at the remaining Land Rover. There was still a problem. Too many people for one vehicle to make it. The extra load would slow them down drastically. Before he could think about it, Sharif Mamud stepped over to sit beside Sims.

"I think that this is a good place, Mr. Sims. Like you, I have no great love for mechanical things. They weary me and put many aches into my ancient bones. I believe I will rest a while with you." He looked up at the canyon walls, raw, ragged, as old as the Sahara. "Yes, this is a good place to rest." He jacked a round into the chamber of his Mats-49 and faced to the south.

There was silence from the group, a feel of awkwardness. No one knew exactly what to say.

Another figure joined the two. Dominic coughed, wiping away a fleck of blood from his lips. He said nothing but his intent was clear. He, too, had picked his time and place to die.

That was enough. Abdul started to step forward. Langers stopped him.

"No more." Abdul's dusty black face began to tighten.

"No more," Langers repeated. "It would serve no purpose save death, and you are not ready. They are. Don't go where you are not wanted, Abdul. This is their moment. Yours will come, but it is not now."

Dominic smiled. "He is right, Abdul. And he may need you later. Get the rest of what you need off the broken Land Rover and put it in the other one. Leave us some ammo and a bit of water. I don't think we will have time to eat dinner. Oh yes, find us some bottles. I know Gus will have a few stashed and we could use a gallon of petrol. That will be all we need. But make it quick." He nodded to the south at a spiral of dust rising around the bend of the canyon.

"You heard him. Let's do it!" Langers commanded, breaking the tension with a direct order. Now there were six: Langers, Abdul, Roman, Gus, and the young couple. It would be crowded but they had a chance if they left now.

To keep Gus from getting too sentimental, Langers had him go to work on storing the extra water and ammo on the remaining vehicle. It was time to leave. If they waited any longer, then they took the chance of losing their only way out.

Moving up to the three, Langers knew that what they were doing was right, and he envied them their death. What more can a man do than pick his time and place to die and know it was right. Dominic had been in the process of dying for a long time. His soul had been leaving him in tiny pieces for years. Sharif Mamud was old, wishing to return to the past of his fathers. This was the place where he belonged. And Sims, well, he was just being practical. If there'd been any other way, he'd have made the little Englishman get back in the Land Rover. But there wasn't. Sims was right. You could see it in his eyes. He was badly hurt. There was no way he could survive the journey back to the Ahaggar Mountains.

The girl and her husband watched in fascination. It was alien to everything they had ever learned. The girl wanted to say something to force Langers into taking them along even if it meant

overloading. It wasn't the expression on his face
that stopped her words, it was that of the three
men. The old Arab, Sims, Dominic, all of them.
Their faces were at peace. There was no fear in
them. If anything, they looked a bit anxious, as if
they wanted the rest of them to get loaded and go
away, leaving them to finish their business. Taking her hand, her husband led his wife over to the
Land Rover.

He said, "I know. Let's just let them do things
their way. This has nothing to do with us."

She knew he was right. Even though the three
had come to rescue them, it had been for their own
reasons. She and her husband had been incidental.
For these men it had been just a job.

Gus took the wheel. He and Dominic gave each
other a long look. Dominic nodded his head up
and down as if to say it's okay, then turned his
back on the Land Rover and looked to the south.
Gus's face was stone. For once he had no quick
words. Carl took the seat beside him. The rest
piled in as best they could in the back, Abdul
facing out the rear with a rifle.

It was hard to leave them but it had to be done.
Fate always dealt all the cards and no matter what
kind of hand you held, when she wanted to, she
would always win.

That was it. They pulled out, heading deeper
into the canyon.

Sunni Ali had his half-track come to a halt.
Taking his field glasses he looked ahead. The men

he was chasing had cost him much. They were not to be underestimated. Adjusting the focus, he brought the abandoned Land Rover into clear view. The doors were open, the spare fuel cans were gone, no one was in sight. Carefully he scanned the gorge on both sides. Nothing. If they had all transferred into one vehicle then he would catch them. Still he felt uneasy, but there was no time left to play a waiting game. He had to go on.

Behind their cover Dominic finished stuffing rags into the necks of three petrol-filled bottles. The half-track would have to pass the Land Rover on the right side. The other side was too rocky. When it did pass and they could hit it with Molotov cocktails, it would block the pass, buying the others a bit more time.

He could see Sunni Ali searching the terrain with his field glasses. Dominic hunched a little lower behind his rock. Patience. They would come to him. The sound of the half-track whiffing into gear brought everyone's head up a bit. Sims moved to where he could set the LMG up, using a rock as a bipod. Sharif Mamud stayed where he was. The range would be too far for his SMG to be of much use until the enemy was near the Land Rover. Overhead the sun hammered at them. Flies buzzed trying to suck moisture. Lizards and serpents observed the proceedings with expressionless eyes.

Sunni Ali signaled for his vehicles to move out slowly. The half-track edged closer to the Land

Rover. His fingers tightened on the trigger of his
MG-34. His eyes were eager. Somehow he knew
that there were men in the rocks around him. He
couldn't see them, he could feel them. This was a
killing zone and he had to go through it. That was
good. The tension, the quiet was good. It fed his
soul. The Tuaregs sensed his feelings. Their dark
eyes also scanned the rocks, hands tightening on
their weapons.

The half-track dug its treads into the rocky
path, grinding over a road that had once been a
trail for caravans. Sunni Ali motioned to the two
jeeps behind him. Obeying, the Tuaregs off-
loaded and spread out, packing the vehicles. If
they were ambushed, he didn't want his men
bunched up where they could be taken out by a
single blow.

"Goddamn that son of a bitch, he must have
read my mind," Dominic grumbled to Mamud.
He had to choke back a cough. His lungs were
filling with heavy black blood, making it even
harder to breath in the furnace air of the canyon.

Crawling closer to Sims he whispered, "When
they get close enough, Mamud and I will heave
the cocktails at the half-track. When we do, lay
fire on the Tuaregs out of the jeeps. They'll be the
hardest to hit later. Then cut loose on the jeeps and
knock them out. If we can do that, there'll be no
way they'll ever catch up to Langers and the
others."

●   ●   ●

"Right you are, love. That's just what we'll do." The sun had reached its apex. Brushing flies away from his mouth and eyes, Sims remarked drolly, "You know, I'll be glad when this is over. It's getting beastly hot. Most uncomfortable."

Mamud and Dominic grinned through cracked lips at the little man's humor. Dominic patted him on the shoulder. "Sims, you might be queer, but you've got more balls than anyone I ever met. It's a pleasure and honor to die with you."

Sims blushed. "Why, thank you, and the feelings are mutual, I assure you. But now we had better keep an eye on those gentlemen below or all our efforts will have been for naught."

He was right. Sunni Ali in his trundling armored beast was almost at the Land Rover.

Flicking his lighter into life, Dominic grinned. "In case I don't have time to say it later, good-bye Sims, Sharif Mamud." He lit the gas-soaked rags.

"Go with God my friends. *Allah maak.*" Mamud took one of the torches. Dominic lit the last one. Holding one in each hand he peered over the rocks. The half-track was there.

"*Now!*" Dominic cried, tossing the two petrol bombs in an overhand arc. Mamud followed with his as Sims opened up with the machine gun, sending a stream of bullets out to hunt down the Tuareg flankers.

Sunni Ali saw the fire bombs as they arced in the air, trailing a dark plume of smoke. Without even thinking about it he reacted. Throwing his

body out of the half-track on the far side, he hit the
ground rolling. He was twenty feet away when the
first bomb hit the open back of the half-track,
exploding among the men there and setting them
on fire.

The next hit the hood of the half-track, bursting
into flames. The liquid fire spilled onto the driver,
bathing his face in flames. In his pain, he released
the steering wheel to tear at his eyes so he could
quench the fires eating at them. The half-track
rolled up against the Land Rover and ground to a
halt. Some of the flames found their way inside
the motor, burning wires and melting fuel lines. In
seconds the entire machine was on fire.

Only the shotgun rider escaped death. He had
covered his eyes with an arm when the bomb
exploded. Screaming, he broke out into the open,
jumping from the cab and rolling on the ground to
smother the fires consuming his robes.

Sims had taken out two of the flankers when he
opened fire. The driver of the trailing jeep went
instantly into reverse, racing his small machine
back behind the cover of the curve in the road. The
other was rendered useless by a burst of machine
gun rounds to the radiator. It would go no farther.

The Tuaregs had reacted quickly by hitting the
deck, seeking cover, and immediately returning
fire. Sunni Ali ran from his exposed position by
the burning half-track and joined them, taking a
rifle from one of his men and giving him his
pistol. "Stay with me," he ordered. To the rest

he cried, "Spread out and keep firing. Leapfrog
forward." To the man with him he asked,
"Where is the tube?"

"In the rear jeep, master."

"Go for it. Bring it to me. Run and we will
cover you.

"Listen to me," he commanded his men.
"They are in the rocks to the left of the half-track,
about twenty meters up. When I say to fire, aim
there even if you can't see anyone. I want you to
keep them down. There can't be too many of
them." He waited to make certain his words were
understood by all.

"Ready. Open fire!"

The Tuaregs cut loose with all they had. Sunni
Ali slapped the man on his shoulder. "Go!
Now!" The Tuareg obeyed. He hunched over as
he raced back to where the rear jeep was sheltered.

Sparks bounced off granite, ricocheting as they
sought softer things to touch. One of them buried
itself in Sims's good leg, fracturing the femur.

Sims cursed, "Now that tears it! My last good
trouser leg shot to hell." He raised up and returned fire, hitting another Tuareg lying in a prone
position behind a clump of dried brush. He was
right on target. The stream of bullets walked down
the man's back, beginning at his neck and ending
at his pelvis.

Sunni Ali picked his targets carefully, trying to
bounce rounds off the rocks where they would
have a chance of hitting the ambushers. A scuf-

fling by his side let him know that his man had returned from the jeep, carrying with him what he had been sent for, an American bazooka and a bag of rockets for it.

From where he was positioned, it would take sheer luck to fire a round that would do much damage, and he didn't have any ammo to waste. He had to get to where he could get a clear shot at them.

"Cover me. Draw their fire. When I move, I want all of you to attack. Move forward to the ditch twenty meters ahead and take cover. When you do, keep firing. I am going to try and get above them."

The Tuaregs moved out, firing as fast as fingers could pull triggers and change magazines. Hundreds of bullets bounced off the rocks, forcing the trio to keep their heads down. Sunni Ali jumped, rolled, crawled, and dodged from one shelter to the next, always heading up, clambering over rocks like a North African mountain goat. He scratched, clawed, and pulled his way over the burning stones till his fingers bled where fingernails had been torn loose.

Three more of his men died in their advance. He was being bled dry. He had to get them now. If he could get back to the jeep with the other radio in it, he could still catch the raiders by calling ahead to have them intercepted.

At last he was above them, resting in a ring of boulders. Peering between two rocks he could see who was holding him up and costing him so many men. There were three of them. It looked like two of them were wounded. He tried to judge the distance and glide factor. He was firing downhill so there wasn't too much to compensate for.

Shoving a round into the tube, he pulled the arming cord on the rocket and set it to his shoulder, making sure the back blast had a free path. He sighted on the target, his eye firmly against the rubber housing of the sight, and pulled the trigger. The rocket left the tube, traveling nearly in a straight line. Dominic saw it coming.

"Take cover!" he cried. He and Sharif Mamud were able to find partial protection but Sims couldn't move. Undaunted, Sims turned his back on the missile heading for him, and calmly shot another Tuareg in the head. At the very same moment the missile struck three feet away from him, tearing his body nearly in half. Splinters hit Sharif Mamud and Dominic.

Another round from Sunni Ali blasted a chunk of meat the size of a pear from Dominic's thigh. He didn't move. Neither did Sharif Mamud. Sunni Ali rose. He couldn't see but he signaled his men to advance. Perhaps one of them was still alive and could be questioned.

Two of his men scrambled up the rocks, leaping over the boulders where the ambushers lay. When the first man came over, Sharif Mamud rose with his knife in his hand crying "Allah akbar" and sunk it to the hilt in the man's chest. Reaching the heart, he tore it in half. The other Tuareg shot the old man in the throat, then crawled over him in time to meet Dominic coming up from behind his rock on one knee, pistol in his hand. He and the Tuareg fired at the same time. Sunni Ali could see the bullets strike as puffs of dust rose from their bodies. Both went down.

Leaving the bazooka, Sunni Ali climbed down to examine them. He had an urge to look at them up close. Once he was on the same level with them he strode over to examine them, his robes flowing loose in the dry breeze. One at a time he turned each of the bodies over to look at the faces. First was the old Arab. He didn't know him, but vaguely wondered why one so old would go on such a hard mission. Next was the small man with the soft face and delicate hands. He had fought well. His body seemed even smaller close up. There was something about death that lessens one. There was also the dark one which his man had shot, putting at least four rounds in the chest and stomach. It had slammed him up against a boulder. Sliding off it, he had gone to his knees, face to the earth like a good Moslem at his prayers.

Stepping over the body of Sims, he saw that his rocket shell had torn a hole the size of man's fist in the other man's body. There were also several holes where bullets had exited. The blood was already turning dark brown as it dried. Flies had begun to gather in swarms on the dead men's wounds, forming black moving clots.

Sunni Ali bent over to grab the dark man by his tunic. He wanted to see this one's face, also. It was important to him to see each of them in order to understand why they had chosen to stand and die, for surely they had known that death would be their fate.

Shoving the body to where it would roll over on its side, Sunni Ali tried to jerk back his hand instinctively but it was caught. Held.

Dominic pulled Sunni Ali to the earth with him. His face was covered with a fine layer of dust. Blood mottled and dried on cracked lips, he was a picture of hell. He had the face of a *djinn* or a madman. Only his eyes were sane. He held Sunni Ali close to his face, holding him down under him. Sunni Ali yelled for help as he struck at his captor's face with his fist. The creature holding him laughed, hacking out blood clots from his ruptured lungs.

Sunni Ali had one quick look before he felt a strange, hard weight on his chest. The creature had stuffed a hand grenade in his jellaba. Frantic, he tried to gouge out the devil's eyes. But it would not let go. He had only seconds before the grenade would explode. His hand slid his curved dagger from its ornate sheath held in the waistband of his robes. Once! Twice! A third time he sank the knife full to its hilt in the maniac's side, back, and neck, but still it would not let go.

Their time was up. Dominic's hands loosened a split second before the blast. He smiled at Sunni Ali, who had begun his prayer. ''Allah is God, the only God, and Mohammed is His proph—'' He never finished. The grenade ended his pleas.

The muffled sounds of fighting followed them through the pass. The survivors avoided each other's eyes. Gus drove on, stone-faced. They would not stop till they reached Fort Laperrine in the Ahaggar Mountains. There wasn't anything back there to wait for.

Langers felt numb. It was always this way. Others died but he went on. Dominic, Sharif Mamud, Monpelier, the others . . .

Opening a crusted eyelid, he watched Gus's face for a moment. One day Gus, too, would die. And still he, Casca alias Langers alias . . . would continue. When that day came it would hurt a great deal, for he would truly be alone again.

Outside the Land Rover desert winds whistled, shifting grains of sand. The Sahara waited also, timeless, patient.

Bitterly Langers shook his head to clear it. Men spoke of killing time. That was wrong. It was time that killed. And no one knew that better than Casca Rufio Longinus, or, as he was known to some, al-Kattel—the killer.